A MAN FOR MIA

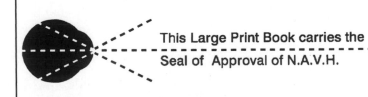
This Large Print Book carries the
Seal of Approval of N.A.V.H.

A MAN FOR MIA

LINDA KAGE

THORNDIKE PRESS
A part of Gale, Cengage Learning

GALE
CENGAGE Learning®

Detroit • New York • San Francisco • New Haven, Conn • Waterville, Maine • London

GALE
CENGAGE Learning®

LIBRARY OF CONGRESS CATALOGING-IN-PUBLICATION DATA

Kage, Linda.
    A man for Mia / by Linda Kage. — Large print ed.
        p. cm. — (Thorndike Press large print clean reads)
    ISBN-13: 978-1-4104-4380-9(hardcover)
    ISBN-10: 1-4104-4380-9(hardcover)
    1. Large type books. I. Title.
PS3611.A34M36 2012
813'.6—dc23   2011039064

Published in 2012 by arrangement with Black Lyon Publishing, LLC.

Printed in the United States of America
1 2 3 4 5 6 7 16 15 14 13 12

For the Boys:

*Glen, Larry, Doug, John, Mark, Ed, Jerry,
Jody, Frank, Lester, V.J., Mike,
Jason, Jerod, Andrew, Jacob J., Cody,
Noah, Adam, Eian, Jacob Roy,
Matthew, Clayton, Benjamin, Gunner,
and of course, for my amazing, most
wonderful husband ever: Kurt Karl.*

CHAPTER ONE

He'd never tried to stop anyone from committing murder before.

It was definitely a nerve-wracking business, Drew Harper realized as he sat tense in the passenger seat of his sister's six-year-old Honda Civic while she blew a four-way stop and careened around a corner, making the tires screech in protest.

He yelped out a curse and clutched the seatbelt strapped over his chest. "What in the world are you doing?"

"I told you not to come," she muttered, her murderous glare fixed steadily ahead.

"Well, what do you expect me to do," he retorted. "When I find you storming out the door with a gun in your hand and muttering something about killing a cheating witch?"

Good Lord, he knew he shouldn't have stopped by her place to raid her refrigerator. But he'd been starving, there'd been no cash in his wallet and his own kitchen was bare of the essentials. And besides, he honestly hadn't expected to find anyone home. His two nieces should be in school, his nephew in day care, and both their parents gone to work. Instead, he'd snuck in the back door to discover Amanda stuffing a handgun into her purse and marching determinedly toward the exit.

"Care to tell me what's going on?" he asked, surprised he was able to sound so casual about the whole situation, when in truth his heart thumped against his ribcage, and he feared he just might have a stroke if his sister blew another —

"Stop light!" he yelled, already bracing himself.

Amanda hit the brake. The seatbelt caught him tight, ripping another stream of curses from his lungs.

"Are you totally out of your mind?" he exploded.

"Last chance to get out," she said from between clenched teeth, sending a meaningful glance toward the curb.

"No," he told her. "Mandy, this is insane. You're a PTA mother for God's sake. What's gotten into you?"

The light turned green. She punched the gas, tearing through the intersection. "Jeffrey's cheating on me."

Drew sucked in a breath. "What?" He knew his brother-in-law looked at other women and occasionally flirted, but touching? He snorted. "No way."

"Way," Mandy growled. Her voice vibrated with emotion and when he glanced over, he realized her entire body quivered from a barely suppressed rage.

He figured arguing with her over the point while she was still in control of the vehicle wasn't smart. So, he more calmly asked, "And you're sure of this because . . . ?"

"Because I'm not stupid," she hissed. "There's a florist charge on the credit card bill. And that jerk never sent me any flowers. He never sent our daughters flowers. I called his mother today. She hasn't received any flowers. He sent them to his little woman. I just know it."

Drew blew out a breath and scrubbed his hand over his face.

Still trying to think up something logical to say to talk her out of, well, whatever she was trying to do, he sucked in a breath when she jerked the steering wheel to the right and slammed them to a stop. Clambering blindly for the armrest, he looked up, only to find them in a peacefully quiet neighborhood with trees lining the street and a pair of young children playing in the yard a few doors up.

"This is it," she murmured, sounding too malicious for his comfort.

Following her gaze to a small light-green bungalow with white trim, he frowned and glanced toward his sister. Her eyes gleamed with an intensity that, frankly, spooked him.

Turning back, he studied the harmless-looking house. "This is what?" he asked. "Who lives here?"

"Her," Amanda breathed the word. "Jeffrey's mistress."

He blinked. "How do you know?"

"Because I visited the flower shop," Amanda answered. "Half a dozen red roses were delivered to this address . . . by my loving, faithful husband."

The loathsome sneer in her voice made the hairs on the back of his neck stand on end. For some reason, he checked the address — 410 South Elm — and envisioned the headlines. *Mother of Three Commits Murder at 410 S. Elm.*

"I can't believe it's true. I can't believe he's really seeing another woman."

Drew came around to find Amanda pulling her purse into her lap and unzipping it.

He reached for the bag. "Mandy," he said, anxiety growing thick in his voice. "Give me the gun."

With a sigh, she shoved the entire purse at him. "Oh, stop worrying. It's not even loaded."

Not taking any chances, Drew checked the chamber. After popping out a live round, he removed the magazine to find it full as well. Arching a look across the seat, he asked, "Not loaded, huh? Then what do you call these? Fake bullets?"

Her jaw dropped. "That jerk. I told Jeffrey not to keep any of his guns loaded with our kids in the house. He promised he wouldn't."

Drew stared at the bullets, wondering what that meant about Jeff's word, when the front door to 410 South Elm came open. Together, both siblings whirled to watch the solitary figure that emerged.

Drew's jaw dropped. "Wow," the word was pulled from him.

But really. Wow.

The woman was slim and small, just the size he liked. No thanks to his parents, he was a tad vertically challenged and felt self-conscious around tall women. He liked being the larger, more masculine half of a couple. But this petite female was, well, she was perfect.

She wore a pair of jean shorts that fit her

slender frame nicely. Quite nicely. They were short enough to show off a good portion of her trim and tanned legs, but equally long to make him yearn to see more. Her short-sleeved top was just as conservative, not so tight he could see every dip and curve, but just enough snug to give him teasing glimpses of the goods, which were very good.

Toting a watering can, she turned her sandaled feet directly to the right after descending the front steps and proceeded to refresh a pair of rose bushes. Drew found himself leaning forward and holding his breath when she paused to bend over and tug a weed from the flowerbed. Though the view of her shorts pulling taut against her backside was too delicious to ignore, the innocent act only added to her wholesome demeanor. She was the ultimate girl next door.

"Not fair," Amanda whispered beside him, sounding devastated. "She's pretty."

Drew guiltily jerked his eyes from the woman. "No," he started loyally. But it was so obviously a lie, his sister speared him with a scowl. "Well, okay. Yeah," he relented. "She's . . . she's really amazing."

"Amazing?" Amanda cried in horror.

He winced. "I mean, she's okay. I've seen

better." On magazine covers maybe. But even as he spoke, his eyes were drawn back to 410 South Elm.

"She looks younger," his sister whined. "I bet she's younger."

Probably, Drew didn't dare concur aloud.

"I just knew he'd find someone younger," Mandy hissed. "The jerk."

It had to be the ponytail she wore. As she crouched down, finding a few more weeds among the roses, the perky bob to her honey brown tresses gave her a youthful presence. She looked too young for Jeff by a good ten years.

That left her just right for Drew.

The dome light in Amanda's Civic came on and the car started to ding as if to warn them the keys were still in the ignition, which only happened if the door was —

Whirling, Drew found his sister sliding one leg from the opened driver's side. Diving across the center console, he grasped her arm, keeping her in her seat. "What're you doing?"

"Let go."

He snorted. "I don't think so."

"Drew." Her tone turned authoritative. "I'm six years older than you. You can't tell me what to do. You never could."

"I'm not going to let you do something

stupid, Mandy. If you get yourself arrested —"

"I'm not going to do anything stupid," she snapped. "Now, let go. I just want to talk to her."

"Says the woman toting a loaded Smith and Wesson."

His sister threw him an annoyed scowl. When she saw the stubborn expression on his face, she growled out a frustrated sound. "Look, I wasn't going to use it. You know me. I couldn't actually shoot anyone."

"Then why did you bring it?"

She gave a helpless shrug. "I don't know. It was just . . . back up. That woman is a complete stranger." She jabbed her finger over her shoulder toward flower girl who was still blissfully tending to her roses. "What if I went to confront her and she turned violent? I want to be able to protect myself."

Drew shook his head, growing more incredulous by the moment. "How were you supposed to protect yourself with a gun you didn't even think was loaded?"

Rolling her eyes, she muttered, "I never even planned on taking the thing out of my purse. Okay? I was only going to wave it around if she came at me."

"Mandy," he groaned, closing his eyes and

running a hand through his hair. "Never point a gun at someone unless it's loaded and you're fully prepared to pull the trigger. What if she'd had her own peashooter stuck in her back pocket and decided to play High Noon? Come on, Sis. Do you know how much trouble you'd be in if you pointed a gun at her? You'd be in jail so fast —"

"Drew," she cut in, sighing as if she thought he was seriously overreacting.

"I'm not joking," he ground out. "Not everyone's as comfortable around firearms as we are. I bet she didn't have a dad as big into hunting as ours. I bet her husband isn't some avid gun collector like yours."

"Probably not," Amanda agreed acidly. "But her boyfriend sure is."

And with that, she tried to exit the car once again.

"Amanda," he warned.

"I just want to talk to her," she repeated.

"And say what? You can't walk up to a person and ask if they're sleeping with your husband. She's not going to just say, why yes I am."

"I don't have to ask," she muttered. "I only have to look into her eyes, and I'll know."

He blew out a harassed sigh. "You're not thinking right. This is absolutely insane."

She turned then and sent him a look that caught him right in the gut. It was heart wrenching and miserable, and he couldn't ignore the pain in her eyes any more than he could ignore his own arm if it'd been ripped off.

"I have to know," she said.

His shoulders collapsed. "Fine," he relented. "But you're not going anywhere. I will talk to her." He stuffed the bullets into his pocket as he added, "And I'm keeping these."

Amanda frowned. "Just what would you say that'd be any different from what I'd say?"

Drew glanced up and down the quiet street, taking in the sight of the two toddlers outside, still playing with a set of toy dump trucks. Even farther up the block, an elderly woman rolled her walker toward a mailbox at the end of her drive. A sprinkler sprayed lazy circles in a yard across the street, and a For Sale sign sat jammed in the grass next door.

"I don't know," he murmured aloud. But he certainly wasn't going to let Mandy reenact her own version of The Nightmare on Elm Street.

Pushing open his door, his gaze settled on the woman. She really was something else.

"Drew," his sister murmured, taking his arm. He paused and glanced back.

She smiled, looking suddenly grateful, and tugged him toward her. "Thank you," she added and slapped a quick kiss to his cheek.

Shaking his head in bemusement, he patted her hand. "Just stay in the car."

"I will. I promise."

Drew shut the door behind him and looked both ways before jogging across the road and stepping onto the walkway that led straight to the front door of 410 South Elm. Not once did he take his eyes off his main objective. As he drew closer, he heard her humming to herself and noticed she wore an iPod. For some reason he smiled, utterly charmed.

She'd already worked her way to the other side of her front door, weeding through a cluster of marigolds.

Taking a moment to study her, Drew licked his dry lips, wiped his moist palms on his blue jeans and spoke. "Excuse me."

The woman jolted, letting out a startled yelp and dropping her watering can, spilling the remainder of its contents. As she spun around, Drew took a quick step backward, hoping to look less intimidating.

Lifting a hand, he sent her his most harmless smile and winced. "Sorry."

She pressed her hand to her chest. As she blew out a calming breath, he stole the moment to study her further.

At this range, he realized the term amazing was actually too mild a description. Her hair was that wispy straight kind that always had a few fly-away strands escape when in a pony tail. Her flyaway strands, however, framed her heart-shaped face perfectly, making her cute button nose look small and adorable and her big grey eyes huge and soulful. Drew drowned in them as they measured him from head to foot.

Finally, her brow wrinkled in question. "Can I help you with something?"

Yes, I'm here to save your life from my gun-wielding sister. "Yeah. I, uh . . ."

Man, if Jeff was seeing her behind his wife's back, Drew was going to kill him. First, for hurting Amanda. And second for taking the only woman who'd been able to make his heart thump this hard in years.

"I saw the For Sale sign over there," he finally murmured, pointing blindly over his shoulder to the yard next door. When she glanced toward the sign, he panicked, thinking he'd lost her attention. "I've been looking for a place to buy lately," he went on and, yes, thank you, her gaze veered quizzically back to him. "And I've found plenty of

18

houses that would do. But none of the neighborhoods have appealed to me yet. This block looks pretty peaceful, though." As long as he kept Amanda off it. "Do you and your husband like living here?" he finished, knowing how subtle he didn't sound, but not really caring. If she was married, he was going to plop down, right there on her sidewalk, and bawl.

At his bold question, she quickly glanced away and blushed. Clearing her throat, she quietly answered, "I'm not married."

Drew sucked in a quick, quiet breath. "Oh," he murmured. "Then this isn't strictly a family neighborhood, huh. Well, that's great. Because . . . I'm not married either."

Yep, still not subtle.

Those big grey eyes swerved back to him. As her gaze flitted down his body, his muscles coiled like a loaded spring. But, wow. If she kept checking him out with those curious yet blushing glances of hers, he was going to do something stupid, like ask her out.

"We have a pretty good mix of neighbors around here," she said. "So, no, it's not strictly a family-oriented community. Though it would be a great place to start one."

Her eyes grew wide after she spoke as if

she realized how leading her statement sounded, like she wouldn't mind starting a family with him.

He grinned. "Sounds like a nice place to settle down."

She bobbed her head jerkily. "Oh, it is. It really is."

"That's good to hear," he murmured. When her cheeks turned pink, he bit his tongue hoping to control his huge, dopey grin.

She was so pretty. And polite. The perfect lady.

As he watched a myriad of timid expressions slide over her face, he got caught in the staring game, studying the shape of her mouth and nose. Her cheekbones. Nearly twenty seconds passed before he realized neither of them were speaking. She was just as busy ogling him as he was her.

Beaming from the inside, he quickly stepped forward and held out his hand. "I'm Drew," he said. "Drew Harper."

"Mia," she returned.

Mia. He liked the sound of that. It was graceful, friendly, and incredibly sexy. Just like the woman.

When she started to lift her own fingers to shake with him, she must've realized they were covered with soil. "Oh," she said, her already pink cheeks turning scarlet. "Sorry. I've been gardening."

"I don't mind," he returned, quickly grabbing her palm before she could pull it away. No way was he going to miss the chance to touch her. "A little dirt won't hurt me."

Her grip was light, but warm and soft. She had slim, delicate fingers. Very feminine. They made his own feel large and male. "It's nice to meet you," they said in unison and then shared an amused smile. She pulled her hand away and self-consciously hid the grubby appendages behind her back.

"Are you just moving into town then?" she asked, nudging the conversation back to distant and polite.

He blinked. "No. I've lived here my entire life."

She tilted her head quizzically. "So . . . you're just tired of where you're living now or what?"

Oops. Caught in his lie, Drew froze, his eyes widening. But he thought up a cover almost immediately. "No. Well, kind of. I've been living in the back of my studio." He shrugged. "But it's getting a little too crowded these days."

"Your studio?" she asked, sounding intrigued.

"Yeah, I . . ." Fumbling for his wallet, he

yanked out a slip of paper. "I'm a photographer," he reported, handing over his business card.

"Really?" she asked on a delighted smile. "That's so neat." Taking the card, she read his address and phone number, running her thumb over the raised script. He sucked in a lungful of air as he watched her caress his Harper Studio logo.

"I always wanted to be one of those freelance photographers," he said, his gaze glued to her fingers as they continued to touch his name, "that traveled the world, you know, and get my pictures on the cover of National Geographic. But my sister lives here and she . . ."

Suddenly remembering Amanda, he did a quick, guilty glance over his shoulder. Did he dare mention her name? If he saw a knowing spark on Mia's face when he said Amanda Wright, then he'd know. But the funny thing was he didn't want to know. If she was having an affair with Jeff, he didn't want to find out just yet and ruin the magical moment they had going.

"It's funny how things work out sometimes," he added on an uneasy laugh, wondering why the heck he was telling her about his big dream to get away and not pushing for the info Mandy needed.

Her eyes lifted from his card. They seemed to see straight inside him. A sympathetic shimmer glittered in her gaze as if she knew exactly how disappointed he was about some of the decisions he'd made in his life.

"I like to tell myself everything happens for a reason," she said softly. "Every tragedy and hardship and letdown is only setting us up for something great farther down the road."

Drew swallowed; the impact of her words hit him low in his gut. She'd lived tragedy and hardship and letdown he instantly understood.

As if realizing she'd gone too deep, Mia forced a quick smile. A self-conscious laugh trilled from her throat, and he swore he could see moisture gathering in her eyes. "At least I hope that's the case," she finished, glancing at him with her top teeth digging anxiously into her bottom lip as if she badly needed him to agree.

"I think you must be right," he murmured and saw the hope she'd mentioned clear in her big grey eyes as if she'd just pinned all hers on him.

It was more than he could take.

Wanting to comfort her and not even sure why, he cleared his throat and glanced away, fighting the impulse. "Anyway, my props and equipment at the studio are starting to spill back into my living space and I thought . . ."

"It was time to expand," she finished on a murmur. Then she smiled, and it was so bright and warm, he wanted to step into her arms and hug her.

She had an incredibly elegant neck. He could picture her tilting it to the side and pushing her silky, straight hair out of the way for the press of a man's mouth. But it wasn't Jeff's head he visualized descending toward that warm pocket of flesh. It was his own.

Clenching his teeth, he glanced away. This was getting out of hand. He'd come to find out if she was Jeffrey's mistress, not to flirt with her himself.

He opened his mouth to speak, but a telephone rang from inside her house, interrupting him.

Mia's eyes widened. "I better get that," she said and started to turn away, only to stop at the last moment. Her smile was hesitant and demure. "I hope everything works out with the house," she told him, glancing toward the For Sale sign.

He nodded. "Yeah. Thanks."

"It was nice meeting you."

"You too."

He remained standing there, watching her scurry up the steps and through the front door. As she disappeared, he ran a hand through his hair and blew out a breath, uneasy about the lies he'd just fed her.

Thinking it was time to get out of there before he made a complete fool of himself and confessed everything, he turned toward Mandy's Civic and jogged his way back across the street.

As he climbed into the passenger seat, he gave the breathless command. "Go!"

Amanda shifted the car into drive and hurried down the street.

Glancing one last time over his shoulder, he took in the fading view of 410 South Elm, dolefully aware he'd never see it or its resident again.

"Well?" Mandy asked.

Drew turned in his seat and stared blankly out the front window. "I think I'm in love."

CHAPTER TWO

"Drew!" Amanda swung an arm out and smacked him hard in the shoulder. "How could you?"

Drew winced and rubbed his arm. "What?"

"That woman is involved with my husband and you —"

"Now, that hasn't been confirmed yet."

"How could you even think about it?"

How could he not?

"Just tell me what happened?" she said, rubbing at the center of her forehead. "Besides you giving her your phone number?"

"I did not give her —" He paused. Oops. "Look. All I did was act like I was interested in buying the house next door. I gave her the business card to let her know I was legit and not some axe murderer stalking her."

"And what did she say to that?"

He shrugged, feeling as he if was betraying some kind of confidence with a woman he didn't even know. "Mandy, I seriously doubt she's seeing Jeffrey, okay. She just . . . she doesn't seem the type. Mia doesn't come across as some kind of mistress. She's too —"

"Mia. Her name's Mia?"

Sighing, he held up a hand. "She didn't put off any vibes that would make me think she'd ever mess with a married man. Okay? She was way too shy and reserved. I'd be more inclined to believe Jeffrey has a thing for her but she doesn't return the sentiment."

"Oh, thanks a lot," his sister groused, pushing a glare his way. "Make my husband look like the bad guy why don't you?"

Drew cringed, realizing he was doing just that. "Maybe he did send her the flowers," he continued anyway. "Maybe he wants an affair." Who could really blame a guy for growing interested in Mia? "But she doesn't seem like the type to date a married man."

Amanda ground her teeth and looked like she might strangle him. But after a thoughtful moment, her shoulders slumped. "So, maybe she doesn't know he's married," she finally relented, looking depressed to admit. "That doesn't mean he's not seeing her."

Drew didn't answer. He didn't want to

believe that scenario. The idea of Jeff any-where near his —

"I should've talked to her myself," Amanda muttered as she pulled into her own driveway and fumbled for her garage door opener.

He glanced across the car to find his sister wiping at her eyes. "Mandy?" he said, re-alizing how inconsiderate he was being. He was such a tactless moron.

She didn't acknowledge him until she'd parked and turned the engine off. Then she twisted to send him a teary-eyed look. Melt-ing, he opened his arms. "I'm sorry. I wasn't thinking —"

"Oh, Drew," she sobbed, hurtling herself over the parking brake. Once he pulled her into his embrace and she rested her head on his shoulder, she sniffed. "What am I going to do?"

He had no idea. He'd never been mar-ried, never even entered a serious relation-ship. And besides, Mandy was always the one he went to for advice. Not the other way around. She never asked him how to handle anything. This was foreign territory.

Smoothing her hair back so it'd stop tickling him in the nose, he asked, "Have you talked to Jeff yet?"

She shook her head, stuffing more curls

up his nostrils in the process, very nearly making him sneeze.

"Well, don't you think you need to address the situation with him?"

Snorting, she answered, "Like he'd tell me if it was true."

Yeah, but . . . "Maybe there really is a good explanation," he tried. "Maybe someone lost a loved one at work and it was his turn to send the flowers. This could mean anything."

"Roses? To someone who'd just lost a loved one?" Amanda asked skeptically.

"Well, maybe —"

"Drew," Mandy cut in, pulling back to frown at him through her raccoon eyes. "You're not helping."

Resisting the urge to wipe at her dripping mascara, he sent her a sympathetic look. "I'm just trying to remind you there are other alternatives. A flower delivery doesn't automatically mean —"

"He won't be with me. In the bedroom."

Well.

That stopped Drew in his tracks. Letting out an uncomfortable laugh, he lifted a hand. "Really, Mandy. I don't need to hear every —"

"Last night," she went on. "I took a bubble bath before bed, put on some slinky lingerie and perfume. For once in my life, I was actually in the mood. But when I kissed him, he pulled away and said he was tired." Giving Drew an intense look, she said, "That's not normal for a guy, is it?"

"Uh." It'd never happened to him before, no. But he'd never been in such a committed relationship before either. As an unattached bachelor, he usually took what he could get when he could get it. "Maybe he's going through a midlife crisis," he suggested.

He wasn't sure why defending his brother-in-law seemed so important. Probably because he didn't want to see Amanda cry anymore. Plus he didn't want to think of Jeff that way. Jeff was as much his big brother as Mandy was his sister. He'd known the guy since he was fifteen. Jeff had coached him through the last part of his puberty, given him advice on girls, and basically acted as his stand-in dad.

He'd say anything to stop the possibility of his sister and brother-in-law splitting up. Anything to give her hope.

"We haven't been together in over three months," Amanda reported despondently.

Drew winced again. But really, did he have to hear about his sister's intimate life?

"I hadn't even realized," she continued,

oblivious to his discomfort. "But yesterday at work, I overheard this woman relaying a date to one of her friends, detailing what this guy had done with her and . . ." she shrugged. "I thought it sounded interesting. So, I wanted to try it with Jeffrey." She wiped at her eyes. "I knew it'd been a while. We're certainly not newlyweds and we do have three children. But, as I was primping, I realized we hadn't done anything since his birthday, which was in the beginning of February. That was a good three and a half months ago, Drew. Jeffrey's never waited three months for as long as I've —"

"Honestly, Mandy!" Drew broke in. "I believe you." Please don't elaborate.

"There has to be another woman," she whispered, looking beseechingly at him as if she needed Drew to do something about it.

Not sure what he was supposed to say, he stared back and dropped his shoulders. The only thing he could think to do was deny, deny, deny. "Maybe he's . . . you know, impotent. I mean, if that were the case, then yeah, of course he'd be too embarrassed to tell you about it. I'd probably stick with the whole I'm-too-tired bit too."

Looking thoughtful, Mandy chewed on her lip. "You think?"

He nodded vigorously. "I really believe

you need to sit him down and have a serious conversation. What you did today was crazy. You've been married to this man for . . . how long now?"

"Twelve years."

"Twelve years!" Drew supplied, sounding incredulous. "Don't you think you owe him the benefit of the doubt?"

Amanda blew out a long, depressed sigh. "But something's wrong, Drew. I just know it. I can feel it every time he's around. Something is wrong."

"Then go to him and find out what it is," he urged, taking her hand and hoping this was the best advice, because if Jeffrey really was sleeping around, Drew was going to have a few words of his own with the dirt bag.

For twelve years, Jeff had kept Mandy happy enough. That was all that mattered to Drew. But Mandy didn't look happy now. She looked heartbroken.

Since she was blood, he picked sides without even thinking. In the blink of an eye, his view of Jeff changed. No one hurt his sister and got away with it.

Reaching out, he smoothed out a piece of hair sticking to her forehead. "Why don't you go inside and take a nap."

She shook her head wearily. "I can't. The

kids —"

"Don't worry about them. I'll pick everyone up from school and day care," he offered. "We'll go out for ice cream or something. Just come get them at my house whenever you're better. You need some time to put yourself back together."

"What? Am I a mess?" Instinctively, she glanced in the rearview mirror. When she saw the black blotches under her eyes, she groaned.

As he watched her wipe with a vengeance, he said, "I'll keep them until Jeff gets home and you've talked to him."

Mia hurried back toward the front door as soon as she hung up with the telemarketer. Anxious to return to the man calling himself Drew Harper, she pushed through the screen and immediately slowed to a disappointed halt.

He was gone. It was like he'd never even been there.

Hopeful, she stepped even farther outside and scanned either side of the sidewalk.

When she remembered she still held his business card, she looked down and blew out a relieved breath.

Okay, so he hadn't been a figment of her imagination. At least that was something.

She wasn't turning into a schizo. Always a plus.

But where had he gone? And why had he fled so quickly?

Assuming she'd probably freaked him out by her weird comment about every tragedy happening for a reason, she groaned. How lame could she get? Finally, there'd been a guy looking at her like she was a normal, average woman, like a woman he could become interested in, like there was nothing wrong with her. And for a brief moment, she'd actually felt like that woman.

She wasn't though. Not by a long shot.

After attending an appointment with her grief counselor, Mia was glad she'd already decided to take the rest of the afternoon off work.

Dr. Higgins hadn't been so patient and understanding today, though his voice had been kind enough and his face full of compassion when he'd said, "Mia, you've been coming to me for a year now. I think it's time for us to progress to the next step."

His words induced her heart to thump rapidly against her ribcage. Her hands clenched instinctively in her lap. Panic rose in her throat and her breathing escalated. With no idea how she managed a calm façade, she licked her dry lips and asked,

"Wha-what's the next step," though, honestly, she already knew.

She knew every step, had learned and memorized them to the point she could write the entire grief booklet herself. She could even tell which step she was caught on.

Acceptance. The last and final stage. It snagged her every time.

Like clockwork, she'd wound her way through the other four and passed each milestone, silently but steadily plodding forward.

But moving on with life, admitting she was a real person, becoming whole again, accepting. That was her ball-dropper every time. She couldn't stop the anxiety clogging her veins whenever she tried to tackle that particular goal. And how could she? It was her fault her baby was dead, her responsibility to make sure Lexie —

Refusing to go there, Mia brought up a picture of Drew Harper in her mind and sucked in a calming breath.

What had it been about him? They'd barely spoken for five minutes. But out of nowhere, there'd been this guy with dark, curly hair who needed to shave, looming in front of her. And tackling step five suddenly didn't seem like such a big deal anymore.

No one had ever, ever, made her feel that cured before.

But now he was gone, the moment passed, and she was still miserable Mia Stallone, stuck on the last step of bereavement and forever guilty over killing her infant daughter.

As she picked up her fallen water can, a red convertible zipped into the drive and parked behind Mia's grey Nissan. Tucking the water pot against her ribs, she smiled softly as the dark-headed five-foot-nine goddess sprang from the driver's seat

"Hey, chickie," her roommate called, grinning as she bound toward the entrance. "You're home early."

"I took the afternoon off," Mia answered, jealousy nibbling at her. But how could she help it? Piper was so vivacious, happy. Alive. "I had a meeting with Dr. Higgins today."

Piper's smile faltered, but she didn't let it waver long. Eyes flickering with curiosity, she asked, "How'd that go?"

Mia nodded. "Good." After giving her usual answer, her roommate didn't ask anymore about it.

Instead, Piper paused and took in Mia's face, frowning thoughtfully. "Hmm," she murmured.

"What?" Mia said, growing uncomfortable under her friend's intense inspection.

"You're . . ." Piper scowled harder as she scratched at her scalp. "Well, if I didn't know any better, I'd say you were glowing."

Mia swallowed, and her face heated as a vision of Drew Harper flared through her.

Piper's jaw dropped. "Oh, wow," she murmured in astonishment. "What happened? Did your appointment with the therapist go that good?"

Blushing even harder, Mia shook her head. "No, I . . ." She had to glance away as she mumbled, "I just met a guy."

Piper froze. Her eyes widened fractionally. Shaking her head she said, "I'm sorry. You what?"

Mia grinned, suddenly very light and animated.

"Oh . . ." Piper whispered. "Oh! That's wonderful." Leaping into action, she pulled Mia into a hearty hug, holding her tight. She smelled of the beauty salon where she worked.

As the aroma of hair dye and perming solutions enveloped her, Mia stood absolutely still, trying not to let the contact bother her. She hadn't enjoyed hugs since the tragedy. People who slept on while their child suffocated to death didn't deserve to be hugged. Though she couldn't take it any longer, she bit her lip and refused to squirm, hoping she didn't insult her friend by pulling away.

Thank God Piper sensed her tension. Quickly stepping back, she gasped, "Sorry." She apologetically patted Mia's arm and retreated even more, giving Mia space.

"No, I'm sorry," Mia started. "I —"

"Stop apologizing. Just . . ." Piper waved her hands, exuding impatience. "Tell me about this guy."

Mia blew out a breath. "His name's Drew."

"Drew." Her roommate grinned. "I like it. What's he look like? Where'd you meet him? Did he ask you out?"

Swept into Piper's excitement, Mia laughed and pressed a hand to her racing heart. "No, he didn't ask me out. I barely said hi to him. Actually, I think I scared him off with my . . . my behavior. But talking to him felt so . . ."

She sighed as energy burst inside her. Something that had lain dormant in her for over three years bloomed into fulfillment and sparked her skin with blissful tingles. It'd been so long, she was almost scared of the sensation.

"You don't need to say any more," Piper murmured, reaching out to grip her hand.

"You felt. That's something right there."

"Yeah," Mia agreed. She tried not to be conspicuous as she pulled her fingers free. "That's something." Dr. Higgins would be proud, anyway.

Vibrating with enthusiasm, Piper laughed and asked, "So . . . does this mean you might want to go out with me to the club tonight?"

"Oh!" Mia laughed. "No. No, I don't think so. If I try too much progress in one day, I might short circuit and digress."

Piper continued to smile, but Mia could see the disappointment in her eyes. She bit the inside of her lip, wanting to apologize. But Dr. Higgins' words glimmered through her head. Don't apologize. You have every right to be exactly as you are.

"I'm really proud of you, you know." Piper flashed her a grin. "This was an improvement . . . no matter how small."

"Thanks," Mia murmured, still guilty for turning down her friend's offer.

But Piper wasn't about to let her worry about it. Wiggling her eyebrows, she followed with a wink. "And with that, I'm going to hit the shower and get ready for tonight. If you want, I'll make a toast with my crew for you."

Mia grinned. "Sure."

"You're doing great." Piper unconsciously reached for Mia, but realized what she was doing at the last moment and dropped her hand. Rolling her eyes at her own thoughtlessness, she grinned and headed toward the steps to enter the house.

Mia lingered outside, hugging the watering pot to her chest as she watched her friend go. She shook her head and let out a small sigh.

Two steps forward and one step back.

She glanced down the street both ways, hoping Drew Harper just might reappear. She owed him a big thank you for making her pulse race and her adrenal glands surge. It'd been way too long.

When she actually saw a car turn onto her quiet street and start her way, she sucked in a breath. It slowed as it neared her drive. Clutching the watering pot in a death grip, Mia strained to see who operated the vehicle. The driver pulled to the curb, cut the engine, and swung the door open.

When a middle-aged woman exited, Mia's shoulders gave, and she started to turn away. But the woman in the tan power suit moved so determinedly toward the For Sale notice next door, Mia found herself watching curiously. Something tucked under the stranger's arm caught Mia's attention until she realized it was a "sold" sign.

The woman pulled it from her armpit and set it snugly on top of the for sale sign.

For a moment, Mia couldn't breathe.

He'd bought the house? Already?

Wait. There was no way he could've bought the house so soon. She'd only spoken to him a few minutes ago. There'd been no time. And besides, he hadn't even looked at the inside.

Disappointment surged through her. He wasn't going to be her new neighbor.

As if she felt eyes on her, the real estate agent glanced Mia's way and sent her a small nod of greeting.

Mia swallowed, suddenly ill. "It's sold?" she lifted her voice, asking the obvious.

"Sure is." The saleswoman strolled toward her. "And to the cutest family you've ever seen. Mom, dad and two perfect children. First time buyers."

Looking down at her hands, Mia murmured, "There was a man here a few minutes ago, checking out the yard. He . . . he said he was thinking about buying this place."

"Well, I have half a dozen others for sale just like this one if he's interested." The woman whipped a pamphlet from her pocket. Her eyes glowed intently, ready to

41

make another sale.

"Actually, it was more the neighborhood than the house itself he liked," Mia explained.

"Oh, sure, sure," the saleswoman said. "I understand that. And I have other places for sale at addresses just like this block." She reached into her pockets again, but came up with nothing. Biting her lip, she frowned and lifted a finger toward Mia, silently commanding her to hold on a second. "Let me jot down a few of them and if he stops by again, you can give him the list. Okay?"

"Uh . . ." Mia realized she didn't have much choice in the matter as the agent scribbled madly on the back of her first pamphlet. "Okay," she murmured. "If he comes back."

But even as she said the words, her fingers contracted around the business card still tucked in her hand. It'd grown damp from her sweaty grip, but she continued to hold it, wondering why wait until he did or didn't come back?

What if she took the addresses to him?

CHAPTER THREE

When Mia saw the house, she almost wrecked. It was spectacular. Pressing on the brake before she ran into a ditch, she peered out the front windshield.

Her lips parted in awe. "Wow."

At first, she couldn't believe Drew Harper actually lived here. But she double-checked the dog-eared business card and, yes, all the numbers corresponded. Besides, it was impossible to ignore the Harper Studio sign in the front yard that matched the logo on his card.

Located on the outer edge of town, the two-story farmhouse sat, surrounded by pastureland on both sides. A herd of cattle grazed lazily, lifting their heads to stare at her as she pulled into the drive. A small grove of fruit trees made up his back yard and someone had planted sunflowers in the field across the street. In full bloom, their beaming yellow and brown faces brightened the already sunny blue day.

As a whole, the place enticed her.

Someone — Drew, no doubt — had taken care of the old home. The white siding and blue shutters looked freshly painted. The grass was mowed short and the shrubs trimmed neatly, welcoming her.

Her smile faltered. Why would Drew want to leave a place so amazing? Why would he look for somewhere else to live?

Biting her lip, she parked and cut the engine.

It'd taken her twenty-four hours to work up the courage to come. And now that she was here, the trepidation mounted even stronger.

This was insane. The man had probably already forgotten their brief meeting yesterday. He'd probably already forgotten her. She should just go home and forget ever meeting him. Besides, it wasn't like she could do anything with him even if he did return her interest. If he asked her out, she'd probably just say no. And if she did manage to accept, the date would no doubt totally bomb. Then she'd be forced to tell him —

Mumbling under her breath, Mia turned the car back on and closed her eyes. Fighting the depression swamping her for chickening out, she curled her fingers into fists and jerked her eyes open when paper crinkled in her grip. She looked down at the tattered business card.

She'd slept with the silly thing, clutching it to her heart all night. Dr. Higgins would probably drop her flat if he discovered how obsessive and neurotic she'd become.

Pathetic as it was though, Drew Harper's business card gave her hope. It reminded her of the way he'd made her pulse race. If she left now, she feared she might never feel that alive again. Whimpering out a moan of distress, Mia turned off the car and pushed open the door. She studied his assortment of flowers as she slowly made her way to his covered porch, thinking she could stay busy with a yard this spacious. She'd have fun nurturing those irises and tulips. She'd probably have to add some roses, though. A flower garden wasn't a flower garden without roses, after all.

Realizing she'd just pictured herself living here, adding to his garden, Mia bit her lip again and forced the image from her head.

She stepped onto the veranda, refusing to think how nice it'd be to sit on the swing in the corner on a nice summer evening and watch the sun set.

The main door hung open in friendly

reception, and Mia's nerves settled some as she knocked lightly on the screened partition.

"It's open," a man's voice — Drew's voice — called from deep inside the house. "We're in the studio. Come on back."

Mia winced. *We? The studio?*

Oh great, he was working. She hadn't realized he'd be taking pictures on a Saturday. Not wanting to bother him while he was with a customer, she hesitated. But he'd already invited her in — it'd be rude to flee now — so she blew out a breath and stepped into the parlor.

The wooden floor made her footsteps echo as she crossed the threshold.

She could immediately tell this was his place of business. Huge framed portraits flooded the walls and floor.

Curious about his aptitude, Mia lingered in the front room, studying his work.

The man had talent. Every shot seemed to catch its main subject in exactly the right pose. She grinned at the portrait of a toddler wearing nothing but a diaper, laughing as a Dalmatian licked his face. But when voices drew near, she pulled away from the photograph and hurried around the corner to join them, almost colliding with a woman toting a baby on her hip.

"Oh." She jerked to a stop and pressed her hand to her heart.

"Sorry about that," the woman apologized. "Didn't see you there."

From behind her, Drew's surprised voice said, "Mia?"

Mia glanced at him but her gaze was immediately drawn back to the child. Her vision blurred, and suddenly she couldn't breathe so well. White, hot panic pressed against her lungs; she feared she might pass out.

But, it was a baby. She was less than three feet away from a tiny, little —

The infant gurgled on his slobber and grinned at her, reaching out a chubby hand.

Sucking in air, Mia blinked the boy back into focus. He was around half a year old with full cheeks, a thin layer of white-blond hair and bright blue eyes.

Before she realized what she was doing, she smiled. Her chin trembled; she had to bite the inside of her lip to keep tears from misting her eyes. Ignoring the emotional meltdown transpiring inside her, she held out her own finger and the baby eagerly clamped his fist around it. He giggled, and her smile grew.

Drew chuckled. "I told you he was going to be a flirt, Mrs. Franklin." He winked at

Mia and slid his gaze to her finger still tightly gripped in the infant's fist. "See there. The kid already knows when he has the attention of a pretty lady."

Mia's face heated. Mrs. Franklin tucked her son close and beamed. "I have a feeling he's going to take after his father in that regard," she announced with a reluctant grin.

Behind them, a computer on Drew's desk chimed and a small panel slid open, offering a CD. Turning, Drew murmured, "There we are," as he extracted the CD from its tray and reclosed the door.

CD in hand, he moved to his printer where a label sat, already printed with the date and the name *Franklin* typed on it. Peeling it from its backing, he neatly pasted the label to the surface of the CD and eased the finished product into a paper slipcase advertising the Harper Studio with its logo splashed across the front.

When he finished, he turned back to Mrs. Franklin. "Here are your proofs."

Mesmerized, Mia watched him. His careful attention to detail impressed her; she found herself watching his long fingers as he handed the proofs over.

He understood how important the pictures on that disc were to his customer.

They weren't just photos of some nameless kid, but memories that would last for years, even past the boy's lifetime. She had albums full of Lexie's cherubic face.

"Call whenever you decide what you'd like," Drew told his client. "Then we can either set up an appointment, or you can just tell me your preference over the phone." He paused as if trying to remember if he'd left anything out of his spiel. Then he lifted a finger and grinned. "I gave you a price list with all the different packages offered, didn't I?"

"You did. Thank you," Mrs. Franklin answered.

"Great. You're all set then." He reached out to cup the side of the child's head, like he was used to handling children, and smiled at the mother. "You and Parker have a good day."

He used his thumb to quickly caress Parker's silky fuzz of hair and then dropped his hand. Glancing briefly toward Mia, he walked Mrs. Franklin to the door.

Mia didn't follow but awkwardly remained where she stood, realizing how big of a mistake it'd been to come. She wondered what would be the best route to escape.

After waving them off, Drew finally turned back to her.

Apprehensive, she stayed rooted to the floor, unable to move. Noticing she'd begun to twist her hands together, she immediately dropped them to her sides.

Something had changed. She could practically taste it. It oozed off him in thick, aromatic waves.

He didn't look pleased to see her. He wouldn't make eye contact. His movements were stuttered, telling her how uncomfortable he felt, and the tightness around his mouth spoke volumes more than anything he might say.

Shrugging as if suddenly self-conscious, he motioned toward the closed door and then jammed his hand into his pockets. "That was Parker." Yanking his hand from his slacks, he tugged at his collar. "He, uh, he was in here for his six-month pictures. His mom seemed happy with the results."

"That's good," she said, feeling lamer than lame. She should go. She should just leave before he —

He cleared his throat. "So . . ." Though she knew his grin was forced, it actually appeared to be genuine. "What brings you by? Decide you need your picture taken?"

"I . . ." Breathe, Mia, breathe. Sucking in a dry lungful, she glanced his way and started over. "You look really busy. I should just . . ." *run for my life.*

She finally moved, stumbling toward the door. But he leapt after her.

"No, wait." When his hand wrapped around her arm, she actually gasped. He immediately let go. "I was just going to say . . . Parker was my last appointment for the day. I'm not busy at all. What can I do for you?"

I need you to help me gain acceptance, she didn't say.

Good Lord, how pitiful was she? If she told him she'd decided he was going to be the one to help her get through her dark patch, he'd laugh her off stage and start zinging tomatoes. She really was pathetic. People didn't make that kind of choice after one brief, meaningless encounter with a complete stranger.

She'd felt something though . . . something cosmic and colossal when she'd turned from her flower bed and first looked into his blue eyes. It'd been so strong, pulsing through her, practically screaming to get her attention. Her senses had started pointing and jumping up and down, doing that urgent pee-pee dance, insisting, "That's him! That's him! He's the one."

Then again, what was she doing, listening to her stupid senses? If she possessed some

51

kind of sixth sense that instinctively knew what was and wasn't, then Lexie would still be alive today.

She swallowed and tried again. "I just came by to tell you the house was sold."

He blinked, looking totally clueless. "What house?"

"The . . ." Another huge gulp. "The house next door," she reminded him. "Next door to me. The one you were looking at yesterday."

Eyes widening, he yelped, "Oh! Right." Then he grinned and smacked the palm of his hand to his forehead. "I have no idea where my mind is. That house. Of course." His brows lowered. "It's sold, you say?"

She nodded. "The real-estate agent stopped by almost as soon as you left yesterday. When she put up a sold sign, I couldn't believe you'd bought it that fast. So, I asked her about it, and she said a family of four had purchased it already."

"Really?" he murmured and scratched the side of his neck. "Well, that's . . . that's too bad. But I'm glad a family got it. I'm sure they need it more than I do. As you can see, I'm surviving here."

As he motioned to the room at large, Mia gazed about her. Surviving? Ha. He was thriving here. Why, in a place like this, she could —

Blushing scarlet for once again thinking about living here herself, she zipped her gaze guiltily his way. Praying he had no idea what was going on inside her brain, she cleared her throat. "She, ah . . . The real-estate agent, that is . . . wrote out a quick list of other places for sale. She swore their neighborhoods were just as nice as ours."

She yanked the addresses from her pocket. Realizing she'd folded the sheet way too many times, she thrust it his way as if to dispose of incriminating evidence as soon as possible.

"Here."

He paused, looking taken aback. "You didn't have to go to all that trouble," he told her, taking the page to slowly smooth out every nervous fold she'd made in order to read the note.

"Oh," she waved an unconcerned hand. "It's okay. I don't mind."

He scanned the addresses briefly, looking like he might actually be reading them, before he lifted his face. "Thanks," he murmured. "I appreciate this."

As he glanced away, something passed through his gaze. Guilt? Regret? She couldn't exactly read the emotion. But it definitely wasn't gratitude. His face had drained of color and he looked sick enough to vomit.

"Well." She self-consciously crossed her arms over her chest and took a step back. "I should probably go."

He lifted his face. "Mia," he started as if he were about to confess something big.

She nodded, urging him to continue.

But before he could say anything, the front door burst open and another woman exploded into the house like she owned the place.

"Drew! I had an idea."

She was older than Mia by five to ten years and had impossibly curly, dark hair . . . just like Drew's.

"Mandy," he said breathlessly and dodged forward quickly, just enough to stand directly in front of Mia, blocking her from the other woman's view.

Whether he was trying to hide or protect her, Mia couldn't tell.

"What are you doing here?" His tone was nervous, his words breathless and rushed.

The woman he called Mandy had been hurrying forward, a flurry of motion. But at his question, she faltered and slowed. Mia peeked around him in time to see her frown in confusion.

"You never ask me —"

That's when she noticed Mia. This time, she came to a shuddering stop. Eyes widening with a sense of recognition, Mandy's jaw dropped. Mia had a split second to wonder why she looked so shocked before that very shock dissolved into rage.

"You," Mandy hissed. Suddenly, she was moving again, stalking with a determined stride, like a bull toward the red flag.

Drew turned to the side so he could face both women, like he knew better than to put his back to either of them. But to Mia, he'd just opened the gate to let the enraged bovine through.

Stumbling backward, away from the woman with murder in her eyes, Mia tripped on a framed portrait that had been resting on a floor easel and went sprawling.

Triumph filled her predator's face. She had Mia right where she wanted her. And she would've gotten Mia too if Drew hadn't stepped between them and caught the charging woman around the stomach.

"Mandy," he said, his voice steady but firm, his arm uncompromising as it hooked her waist. "Stop."

But his stern command only enraged the woman further. Stomping on his instep hard enough to make him grunt, she glared over her shoulder, lashing him with a lethal glare.

"How could you?" She sounded so betrayed and crushed even Mia felt a spurt of outrage on her behalf.

She stumbled to her feet just as Drew yelped, "What? You actually think I invited her here? She just showed up out of nowhere, Mandy. I swear."

Mia frowned, hurt and confused. She was missing something, something huge and important. But what, she had no idea.

"What's going on?" she dared to ask, her voice tremulous and uncertain.

Mandy glared. Trying to leap out of Drew's arms and charge once again, she snarled, "He's married. Do you know that? Do you even care?"

Eyes widening, Mia pressed a hand to her chest, too frightened to even breathe.

"He's married," Mandy bellowed. "To me! And we have three children together. Three beautiful, perfect —"

The rest of her words were muffled behind a door as Drew picked her up and manually shoved her inside, pulling the portal shut and then placing his body in the entrance to bodily block it.

As the trapped woman started to pound and demand her release, screaming, "Drew! Let me out. Let me out right now," he sent a guilty wince Mia's way.

"She'll cool off pretty soon," he assured, though he didn't look too confident.

Mia could only gape. Finally, air exited her lungs and she was breathing again, breathing enough to gasp, "You're married?"

CHAPTER FOUR

The door locked from Mandy's side and no matter how much of his weight Drew braced against the closed portal — which was all of it — his sister still threatened to bulldoze her way out. His body lurched forward a couple inches after one of her mighty shoves.

"Drew! You low-down, rotten man." Mandy's voice echoed all too clearly through the thick wooden panel. "If you want to live through the rest of the day, you'll let me out . . . right . . . now."

"I'll let you out as soon as you settle down."

In answer, she shoved against the door so hard she very nearly succeeded in throwing him off it. What followed was a stream of gutter talk so crude he was shocked to learn his sweet, naive sister even knew such words.

She directed every one of them at him too.

Attempting to ignore her, he focused on

Mia. She stood in frozen horror, gaping at him with one hand fisted to her chest and her big grey eyes blooming wide with disappointment.

"You said you weren't married," she choked out in an accusing voice, looking devastated.

He frowned. "I'm not."

"Drew," his banshee of a sister screamed. "Are you talking to her? Don't you dare talk to that witch. I'll never let you see my children again if you so much as look at her."

Even as Mia took another cautious step back, her eyes narrowed on him. "Well, she certainly seems to think you're married."

"What?" he said, blinking back his confusion. "Mandy doesn't think — Oh. Oh, no. No! She's my sister. I'm not the man married to her."

"Your sister?" Her shoulders slumped in relief, but in the next moment, Mandy started pounding again, making her jump. "But . . ."

"She's my sister," he insisted. To prove it, he slapped the palm of his hand against the door behind him. "Mandy," he called. "Tell her I'm your brother."

"No," Amanda yelled back. "I disown you, you dirty rat. We are no longer related." She shoved at the door, making him grit his teeth against the pain that spiked up his spine.

Sending Mia a rueful smile, he said, "See."

She shook her head. "No, I don't see. I don't understand what's going on at all."

"Let me out," Amanda called. "I'll make her understand."

Mia jerked back at the threat, and Drew lifted both his hands, keeping the door braced with his back. "Okay, here's the deal," he confessed. "I haven't exactly been honest with you."

Mia's lips parted. "So, she is your wife?"

He sighed. "No. She's really my sister. But . . . I . . . She . . ." He closed his eyes and pressed the palm of his hand against his forehead. "She thinks her husband's cheating on her."

"She . . ." Shaking her head, Mia frowned in confusion.

"With you," he finished.

He could tell that caught her completely off guard, and it did his heart good because it upped the possibility she was completely innocent of all wrong-doing.

"Your sister thinks I'm dating her husband?" she repeated slowly like she was sure she'd misunderstood him.

It took him a moment to give the terse

nod, but he did, making her jaw drop.

"Well, let her out. I'll tell her right now I'm not."

He made a pained face. "Ah . . . Right now might not be such a good time."

"Listen to her," Mandy called. "Let me out."

"I'm not dating your husband," Mia stated adamantly, raising her voice so Mandy could hear her. "I'm not dating anyone's husband."

"Are you sure?" Drew asked, mentally kicking himself even as the words spilled from this mouth. "I mean, maybe you don't know he's married."

Letting out an anguished cry of outrage, Mia took a moment to send him a disappointed glare. "I'm positive," she growled from between gritted teeth. Then she spun away and started for the exit.

"Mia!" he called after her, his voice desperate, pleading.

Whirling around, she glared at him. "What made her think I would ever . . ." Too upset to even finish the question, she seethed, pinning him with that same disheartened frown.

Mia wanted to hurt Drew Harper. She also wanted to curl into a ball and weep.

For three long years, she'd been unable to get close to anyone and suddenly, here was this seemingly perfect guy, making her think she might finally be able to heal.

But Drew wasn't what she thought he was. He was a deceiver. A fraud.

"I don't even know her," she said, pointing toward the closed door he held shut with his entire body. "And I probably don't even know her husband."

"His name's Jeff Wright," he was quick to explain. "Jeffrey Alan Wright."

Mia shook her head. The name meant absolutely nothing. "Never heard of him."

Drew nodded, looking relieved. But that only infuriated her more.

"This makes no sense. Why me? Why'd she pick me?"

He glanced away guiltily. "Her husband had half a dozen red roses delivered to 410 South Elm Street."

Mia's eyes flashed wide. She barely managed to keep the gasp of realization in, but she was sure he could see the comprehension in her eyes as all the pieces of the puzzle finally fit.

"What?" he asked anxiously.

Shaking her head, she said, "I haven't received a delivery of roses." And that wasn't a lie. "No one's ever sent me flowers." More truth. Yet, guilt heated her face. She glanced away, only to dart her gaze back to him.

Drew watched her closely, frowning slightly. She could tell he didn't believe her. She bit the inside of her lip, hating the fact she'd never been able to hold a poker face. It was probably the biggest reason she was still in counseling. The doctor could tell too easily she wasn't healed.

"You know something," he pressed.

Yes.

Mia shook her head and turned away so he couldn't see her face. "I have to go."

"Mia," he called. "Please. This is my sister's marriage we're talking about. If you know something —"

"I don't," she cut in, which technically was true. She didn't know. But she could make a pretty accurate guess. "I'm sorry. I can't help you."

And with that, she fled.

Drew probably waited longer than he should've before he opened the door to let Mandy out. But, unreasonably protective of Mia, he didn't move until he heard her car start, giving her a chance to escape.

He still couldn't believe she'd come to visit him or that she'd used such a flimsy excuse as to bring him a listing of houses for sale. It was flattering actually. She'd tried a little too hard to make up a reason to visit.

If she was that interested in him, she couldn't be involved with Jeffrey, ergo, she was free for him to pursue. But then again, if she was dating a married man, she probably had no qualms about seeing other men on the side.

But he didn't think that was the case.

He prayed it wasn't.

When he finally stepped aside and opened the door, his sister spilled through the opening, landing on her knees and catching herself with her hands.

"I guess you heard her answer."

Mandy ignored him. She carefully pushed to her feet and went about wiping floor dust from her knees and palms. When she straightened, her cold gaze slid his way.

"I heard her deny it. But you already said she would. If she was involved with a married man, she'd have no problem with lying."

He shook his head. "I don't think she was lying."

"You can't know that."

He frowned, defensive. "I saw her face, Mandy. You didn't. She was telling the truth."

"Yeah, you saw something on her face," Mandy murmured, scowling at him. "I heard everything you two said. You could tell she knew something."

He opened his mouth, but no words came. Amanda was already mad enough, knowing he was attracted to her husband's possible mistress. It would be in very bad taste to keep defending said accused mistress.

"What're you doing over here, anyway?" he snapped, instead. "Where are your children?"

She scowled. "Jeffrey's mother's taking them to the zoo today. Don't change the subject."

He growled out a grumble of irritation. "She wasn't lying when she said she didn't know Jeff."

"Then —"

"It was the roses," he confessed grudgingly.

Amanda cocked her head, confused. "What about them?"

"Her eyes widened when I mentioned roses being delivered to her address."

"Aha!" Mandy literally leaped a couple inches off the floor as she snapped her fingers. "I knew it."

"You don't know squat," Drew reminded her. "She looked completely blank when I said Jeff's name. She doesn't know him." He ran his hands through his hair. Frustration raced through him like an attack of low-blood sugar, making him jittery and restless. "There has to be some kind of reasonable explanation —"

"Oh, pul-lease. If there was a reasonable explanation, then why didn't she give it?"

Good question. He'd like to know that as well.

Fed up with the entire conversation, Drew threw up his hands. "I don't know! Okay? I do not know. Maybe she was freaked out from you trying to murder her. It'd sure jumble my brains a bit."

Setting her hands on her hips, Amanda's eyebrows snapped together. "Will you stop defending her? It's making me mad. I know she's soooo beautiful, but you best clear that lovey-dovey look out of your eyes fast, buddy boy. You're my brother. Your loyalties lie with me."

As she jabbed a finger into her own chest, Drew arched a brow. "Lovey-dovey look?"

"Don't you dare deny it." Batting her eyelashes, she lifted the pitch in her voice to mimic his words from a few days ago. "I think I'm in love." As soon as she spoke, though, her face pinched tight. She sent him a testy look. "What a bunch of bull. You don't even know her. And worse yet, she'd probably just got done kissing my husband right before she flirted with you."

Drew sighed. "She didn't —" Realizing he was only digging himself deeper, he abruptly stopped trying and lifted his palms in surrender. "Look, I'm sorry for saying that, okay. It was . . . it was stupid, insensitive, and . . . and stupid." Ignoring his sister's snort of agreement, he continued. "But honestly, nothing's been proven yet. I mean, what did Jeff have to say about it?" He paused when she became interested in one of his portraits on the wall. "You did talk to Jeff like you said you would, didn't you?" He hadn't had a moment to discuss the situation with her since she'd come to pick up her children last night.

Mandy swallowed. "Yes."

He frowned, not liking the lump in his gut. "And?"

She avoided his gaze.

"Mandy? You asked him about the flowers, right?"

"Not yet," she mumbled.

"What!? Why not?"

She sighed. "I'm waiting until the credit card bill comes in."

"The credit —" He shook his head. "Okay, you totally lost me."

"Fine. Here's the plan," she started, looking very reluctant to explain. "Jeffrey and I switch every other month to pay the bills. I didn't want to hear him complain when he saw how much I had to spend on Natalie's uniforms for this summer's dance camp. So I went online to make sure my purchase would show up on the month I pay bills. That way he'd never even see how much they cost. But then I saw fifty dollars had been spent at Thornback's Posey Shop, and I almost flipped. I was ready to call the credit card company and report identity theft."

"Fifty bucks for six roses?" Drew echoed in disbelief.

Good Lord. Last time he'd bought anyone a bouquet, it'd been Mandy's birthday and he'd gotten the six ninety-nine special from the grocery store, which consisted of a couple dozen yellow, half-wilted daisies.

Shaking his head, he returned to reality. "So why didn't you contact the credit card company?"

"Because I wanted to find out who'd been using my card more. I went to the flower shop and bugged the owner until she finally pulled the receipt. And right there, with my very own eyes, I saw my husband's signature for the delivery."

Drew winced. That didn't sound good. But it didn't explain everything. "I still don't understand why you think you have to wait until the credit card bill comes in to ask him about it?"

She looked uncomfortable as she answered, "I don't want him to think I was being nosey and purposely checking up on him. I don't want him to think I don't trust him."

Shaking his head, Drew argued, "But you don't trust him, Mandy. And you found out about the flowers by accident. Why does it matter anyway?"

"Drew, I have this all planned out. Okay? Just back off. As soon as the bill comes, I'm going to open it in front of him. Then, as I'm already glancing through it, I'll be like, 'Oh, it's your month to pay the bills, isn't it?' And right before I hand it over, I'm going to pause and frown at the itemized list. 'Hmm,' I'll say, looking confused. 'There's a bill here from Thornback's. Then, I'll innocently glance at him and ask, 'Did you buy anything from Thornback's?' If he says no, then bam, I have him in a lie. If he says yes and the answer is anything different than having six roses delivered to 410 South Elm, then —"

"Yeah, yeah. Bam, you have him in a lie. I got it."

"But if he has some kind of explanation and it meshes with what I already know, then I'll have my answer and he'll never suspect I thought he might be cheating. I don't want him to be mad at me, and knowing I don't trust him would hurt him, Drew. He'd be so upset."

Drew blew out a long sigh, knowing there was no way to talk his sister out of her idea. "So, what did you talk to Jeff about if it wasn't the roses? You said you talked to him."

"Oh, I asked him about . . . you know, his lack of —"

"Whoa. Sorry I asked. I don't need to hear anymore."

"And he said he'd been really busy at work, dealing with a lot of stress," Amanda continued anyway. "Which kind of clears him, but doesn't completely. He's had stress before. And it's only made him want more intimate —"

"Mandy," Drew bit out. "No more. Please."

His sister rolled her eyes. "I figure the only way I can tell for sure if stress is really making him distant is if you talk to him. Which brings me around to the reason I came over." Looking up at him with pleading eyes, she said, "Will you talk to Jeffrey?"

"Me?" Drew shifted a nervous step back, not liking the turn this conversation had taken. "Why?"

"You're a guy. Guys talk about that stuff."

He sputtered in disbelief. "Not to their wife's brother they don't. In fact, the less I know about you two — like that — the better."

"But I think you might be able to get some information out of him I couldn't."

He snorted. "Honestly, I don't think I could."

"Drew. Please. You'll never know if you don't try."

"Mandy," he started uncertainly. But she'd already moved closer and was clinging to his arm.

"Just come to lunch tomorrow," she pleaded. "Maybe get him off alone for a few minutes. And then tell me what you think? Tell me if he's acting unusual. I'll even cook your favorite. Roast beef."

Giving in, Drew groaned out his displeasure. "Fine," he muttered. "But I refuse to ask him about . . . that."

"Thank you, Drew," Amanda exclaimed, throwing her arms around his neck and pulling him tight, stamping his cheek with a

71

quick kiss. "You're the best brother ever. I owe you."

"Yes," he muttered, making a face of displeasure with each loud, smacking smooch she gave. "You do. Big time."

When Mia got home, she hurried in the front door and shut it behind her, leaning back against the closed panel. Pressing a hand to her still-racing heart, she stared across the living room to the table sitting in the kitchen, or rather to the vase full of six long-stemmed roses perched on top of the table.

Eyeing the blood red petals as if they were contaminated, her breathing grew choppy. No way, she thought dizzily. There was no way those had come from a married man. She refused to believe it. She could never imagine her roommate —

Suddenly, Piper appeared, strolling in from the kitchen as she popped the tab on a can of soda. She started to smile until she saw the expression on Mia's face.

Jerking to a stop, her grin fell. "What's wrong?"

Mia shook her head. She couldn't ask. She wouldn't. She refused to pry into her roommate's private life.

In the past three years, Piper had helped

her in her time of need. When Mia was struggling through her darkest hour, contemplating suicide, her friend called from five hundred miles away, as if she knew how desperately she was needed, and she invited Mia to come live with her.

Okay, so invited wasn't quite the right word. She'd ordered.

"Mia, your family's concerned about you. I think every member's called me in the past week, worried sick. This has gone on long enough."

Mia nodded, but she couldn't answer. She knew exactly how long it'd been since burying her baby girl. But she couldn't seem to do anything about it.

"You need to get away from there," Piper insisted. "You need to escape all the memories and just start over."

Start over. The words sent a shiver up her spine. *Start over.*

"You're coming to live with me. That's all there is to it. And you're going to get help. Your family's been too lenient, not pushing you toward therapy. But that's what you need."

Mia wasn't sure what all her friend went through to move her from Illinois, but a month later, she was living at 410 South Elm and all her things had been arranged in her new room. She didn't remember much of the move. Piper must've taken care of everything because Mia had only been along for the ride, half out of it.

Life here wasn't easy though. It'd been good for her, yes. But easy? No. After starting therapy, along came a job and responsibilities. Piper made her take on half the cooking and cleaning, half the laundry, and half the bills. And her friend had been right about starting over fresh. Moving had been exactly what she needed.

She owed her life to Piper. She'd saved Mia. Literally.

"Nothing's wrong," she murmured now, her voice an octave too high. Tearing her gaze from the flowers, she forced a nervous smile Piper's way.

But her roommate was no fool. Setting her pop on the table next to the roses, she started cautiously toward Mia. Mia wrenched a step back, running into the closed door.

Piper stopped. "Mia?"

"I saw Drew again." It was the first thing she could think to say to divert her friend's attention; the words just kind of rushed from her throat.

Surprise and excitement bloomed on Piper's face. "You did?"

Mia nodded. "I went over to his house."

"Oh, Mia," Piper breathed out in awe. "That's so wonderful. What happened?"

Mia winced. "I totally bombed it." And so had he.

Face falling, Piper's features filled with sympathy. "Oh, honey, I'm sorry. You were so hopeful too."

Nodding again, Mia murmured, "There will be other guys." Even as she spoke the words, though, she worried no other guy would ever provide her excitement and comfort, all in one pleasant package, the way Drew had.

Piper grinned. "That's the spirit. And whenever you're ready, I've got a couple dozen to introduce to you."

Mia chuckled and rolled her eyes. "Not yet," she muttered.

"This guy I'm seeing now, for example," Piper continued. "He's got a bunch of hunky, successful, single friends. I'm sure any one of them would jump at the chance to take you out."

Though Mia was dying to ask about this "guy" Piper was seeing, she kept her mouth shut and merely gave the woman a brief smile. All the while, her mind raced.

Was her best friend dating a married man?

Mia couldn't picture it. But then again,

Piper was being surprisingly closed-mouth about her newest beau. In fact, this was the first time she'd actually volunteered information. After Piper had received the roses, Mia had asked, but Piper merely shrugged it off.

"Oh, he's just this guy I've been out with a few times." And then she'd casually changed the subject, asking Mia about her job.

Mia hadn't thought anything of it at the time, even though Piper was always so eager to share information about the men in her life. But now . . . now, everything was different.

"He knows so many people," Piper was still chatting about her mystery man, making Mia's shoulders loosen with relief. Her friend certainly wasn't acting like she was hiding anything now.

"Last weekend, he took me to this fancy restaurant that's, like, three hours away, and all the waitresses and servers there knew him by name. Isn't that amazing?"

Mia was more amazed by the fact he had to drive so far away to take her to eat. Why couldn't he find someplace close? Did he not want to be seen by someone he knew . . . like his wife?

"So . . ." she couldn't help but ask.

"How'd you two meet?"

Piper grinned and flushed like a teenager with her first crush. "He came to the salon, and I cut his hair."

Mia nodded mutely.

"I guess his usual stylist is Darla. But she was out that day, and he had some big meeting, so he popped in for a quickie trim," she winked, "and got me instead."

Mia swallowed, suddenly ill.

"And, oh my God, Mi Mi. Jay has, like, the softest hair ever. I fell in love with his golden locks after the first snip."

"Jay?" Mia echoed. Short for Jeffrey, perhaps?

Piper cleared her throat and glanced away. "That's my nickname for him."

Nodding pleasantly, Mia ignored the ball of anxiety forming in her stomach. "He sounds . . ." *married.*

"Oh, he is," Piper gushed, coming back around with a beam of excitement. "He's absolutely wonderful. He might be a little older but that just means he's settled and responsible and successful. He's not like the immature, inconsiderate losers I've dated before."

Not sure how to respond, Mia could only watch the glow on her friend's face as Piper detailed his many positive attributes. "Jay" supposedly owned a sleek Charger, wore three-piece suits to work and liked Starbucks.

"I think he might be the one," Piper finished on a blissful sigh.

Mia winced; thank goodness her friend didn't notice.

The thought struck her that maybe Piper didn't know. If she didn't realize "Jay" already had a significant other, then it was Mia's duty to tell her. She owed it to her friend to reveal the truth. But if Jay wasn't Jeffrey Alan Wright then Mia didn't want to scare Piper unnecessarily. Trying to be as unassuming as possibly, she asked, "What's his last name?"

Piper turned away slightly to pick her can up. She stalled a few seconds, drinking heartily, staring at her six roses as she set the can back down. Then she turned back to Mia with a frown. "Is it my turn to cook tonight or yours? I can't remember?"

Mia's lips parted, stunned. "Uh . . . It's mine."

"Thank God," Piper went on. "I told a friend I'd eat out with her. We're going to that new deli on the mall."

As she gabbed on, Mia could only stare. She couldn't believe Piper would so obviously evade her question. It was like she was protecting him, which meant she already knew about his marital status.

Piper couldn't seem to look her in the eyes as she talked about the sandwich she wanted to taste test tonight. "It's supposed to have melted mozzarella and this special sauce . . ."

Suddenly feeling disconnected from her friend, Mia eased a step back. Piper was lying to her, or at least she was avoiding the truth.

The realization hurt.

If Piper couldn't share a secret with Mia, then how strong was their relationship . . . really? How long could Mia continue depending on Piper for her emotional support if they couldn't trust each other?

Too dizzy to listen to any more bull, she cleared her throat and turned to go. But at the last second, she spun back. "Is-he-married?" she rushed out the question, making it sound like she'd uttered one word instead of three.

Piper froze, then slowly frowned. "Excuse me?"

"Is he married?" Mia repeated, straightening her spine. "Does Jay stand for Jeffrey Wright? Is his wife's name Mandy? Do they have children together?"

CHAPTER FIVE

Piper's mouth opened, then closed. Then opened again. "I . . . how . . ." She closed her mouth once more. But her eyes were wide with guilt and surprise.

"She knows about you," Mia said, her voice soft. "His wife. Mandy. She knows he sent you the roses."

Piper shook her head a single time to deny it, but then her shoulders dropped. "Oh, no," she whispered and plopped into a chair, staring up at Mia with a bleak expression. "How does she know? How do you know she knows?"

It was on the tip of her tongue to tell all. Reveal Drew's deceit and his involvement in the entire, sordid mess. But at the last second, she held back. Piper hadn't been honest with her recently, keeping a secret as big and awful as adultery, so Mia didn't mind stretching her own bit of truth. Besides, she didn't want to reveal what an idiot she was for being taken in so completely by a liar like Drew Harper.

"She came here," she said. "Yesterday. While you were at work. She accused me of sleeping with her husband, of receiving your roses. She was upset, Piper. She was so upset."

"Oh, no," Piper said again, covering her gaping mouth with both hands. "She came here? What'd you tell her?"

"I told her the truth. I'm not dating anyone's husband."

Piper waved her arms, impatient. "What about the flowers? What'd you tell her about the roses?"

Jaw going hard, Mia said, "I told her she must be mistaken because no one had sent any flowers here."

"Thank God." Pressing her fingers against her temples, Piper sent Mia a tremulous smile. "Thank you, Mi Mi. I owe you big time."

"You owe me an explanation," Mia said, setting her fists on her hips.

Piper's smile died. She eased to her feet. "What do you mean, an explanation?"

"I lied for you," Mia said through gritted teeth. "I lied to an innocent woman while you were out there, with her husband, doing God-knows-what."

81

Her roommate didn't speak, just stood there, looking ashamed as she stared down at her feet.

"How could you?" Mia whispered. "He's married to another woman, made commitments with another woman, had children with another woman. How could you break up a family, Piper?"

"I . . ." Expression going stubbornly shuttered, Piper lifted her face. "He's miserable, okay? He wants to leave her."

"Wants to and will are two entirely different words, Pipe."

Piper ground her molars. "I know, but —"

"There's nothing you can say that will sugarcoat this. You're wrong. You're —"

"I'm in love with him!"

Mia closed her eyes and pressed her hand to her forehead. "Then wait until he has a license for divorce in his hand before you ever see him again."

"Oh, like that's not going to hurt his wife and children if he leaves them for me."

Shaking her head, Mia turned away. "I can't even talk to you."

"Mi Mi, you don't understand. He and I —"

"I don't want to understand this. I don't want anything to do with it. What you're doing is —"

Eyes filling with tears, Piper cried, "Stop. Just stop." Spinning away, she rushed from the room, her footsteps pounding down the hall until a door slammed.

Shaking with too many emotions to name, Mia crumpled into a chair and covered her mouth with her hands.

Sunday afternoon, Drew found himself sitting across a dinner table from his brother-in-law, eating pot roast. To his left, his niece Natalie rattled on about summer camp her parents were finally letting her attend. To his right, her sister Lucy begged to go too. And all the while, their little brother Felix was lost in his own world, making motor noises as he ran his fork through the mashed potatoes, causing gravy to spill and seep into a pile of peas.

"That's enough," Jeff muttered, scowling at the boy.

Next to Felix, Mandy shot out an arm to catch her son's hand. "Eat," she ordered quietly.

Drew glanced from Mandy to Jeff, unable to imagine their lives separate from each other. This right here was who they were. Not so interested in eating either, he glanced toward his nephew.

Felix, who'd gone right back to making a

fort in front of his pile of peas, but was doing it silently, could be a holy terror sometimes. Drew adored that most about the boy though. Mandy and Jeff had let the girls name him, worried they would feel left out with a new baby around . . . and not just any baby, but Jeffrey's long-wished-for boy. So, per Lucy and Natalie, he'd been aptly dubbed after Felix the cat. He seemed to take his mischievous namesake to heart.

As Mandy once again told her son to stop playing, Natalie blathered on. "And I'm going to get some stationery so I can write you guys every day."

"I want some stationary too," Lucy said.

"Honey, you'll get to go to camp in two more years and you'll get some stationary then," Mandy assured her second daughter as she ripped Felix's entire plate away from him.

From the end of the table, Jeff caught Drew's eye. "Always use condoms," he muttered.

"Jeffrey!" Amanda exploded, looking absolutely scandalized as she plopped the plate back in front of her son.

"What're condoms?" Lucy and Felix asked together.

Narrowing her eyes on their father, their mother hissed, "I believe it's your responsibility to answer since you're the one who started the subject."

Husband and wife battled through a brief stare off before Jeff finally slumped with a defeated sigh. Drew, on the other hand, couldn't be happier. This was exactly the nature of their marriage. He'd never understood it, but it worked for them, or at least it had always worked for them before. It felt almost comfortable to watch them snap at each other.

"You're too young to know," Jeff advised his two youngest.

Amanda snorted. "Brilliant answer."

"Well, what did you expect me to say?"

"I know what they are," Natalie bragged as she lifted her nose, looking smug about being the oldest and so much wiser than Felix and Lucy.

"How do you know?" her dad demanded.

"They're —"

"Natalie!" her mother squawked.

"— those ketchup and mustard and salt packages you get at McDonalds when you order a happy meal."

As her two parents sighed out their relief, Drew threw back his head and laughed. A second later, his brother-in-law joined in.

"Yeah, Drew," Jeff chuckled. "Always remember to order extra ketchup."

"It's not funny," Amanda informed the two men.

Though Drew tried to straighten his face, Jeff sent her an irritated scowl. "Oh, relax. It's not that big a deal."

His wife didn't respond. Instead, she sent her brother a telling look. *See what I mean? This is how he's been treating me.*

But Drew didn't see at all. Jeff and Mandy had always been like this. He still remembered the time when they'd been dating. After one thick snowfall, Jeff had spun a few doughnuts in a church's empty parking lot with his Camaro. Drew had loved it, laughing uproariously as he was slung around the back seat. But from her spot in the front passenger's seat, Mandy screamed her head off, demanding he stop.

Snapping at each other was their way of saying *I love you.*

Jeffrey seemed perfectly normal to him. He hadn't said or done anything that was in any way unlike the usual Jeff.

"You want a beer?" he asked as soon as lunch was over and Mandy was clearing the dinner table while the kids played in the back yard.

Drew sent a quick glance his sister's way. He could tell she'd heard her husband's question because she paused briefly in stacking plates and stared hard at the top of the table. She'd murder him if he said no.

"Sure," he answered and followed Jeff through the kitchen and out the side door into a well-kept garage. Jeff's hideout.

As the older man opened the fridge and ducked inside only to appear with two bottles in hand, a pent-up ball of tension loosened in Drew's chest. Amanda had been freaking him out there. He'd actually worried the man who was almost closer to him than a blood brother was ruining his marriage by dating another woman. But this was Jeff as Jeff always acted.

"So, how's the love life, Drew?" he asked as he handed the beer over.

Drew relaxed even more as he popped off the cap and listened to the refreshing hiss of air that followed. Yeah, he was still the same old Jeff. Always wanted to know about everyone's dates.

Snorting, he said, "What love life?" and took a long drink, relishing the cool liquid that slid down his throat. He closed his eyes, trying to ignore the image of Mia that jumped to the front. But too many times, he pictured her standing in his living room and nervously holding out that list of addresses, her big grey eyes wide with uncertainty and hope.

He sighed as he dropped the beer to his side, only to find Jeff standing there, his own bottle still unopened, studying him intently with his arms crossed. "There's this new intern at the office," he told Drew. "She's pretty cute. Smart too. I could set you up if you want."

"Oh, yeah?" Drew asked, trying to hide his interest. Was it Mia? Did she just have a death in the family and Jeff had sent her flowers?

"Where's she live?" he asked.

His brother-in-law threw him a surprised look. "Heck, I don't know. She just started a couple weeks ago. I've only talked to her a handful of times. We haven't exactly exchanged addresses and phone numbers yet."

"She got a name?" Drew wondered.

"Uh . . ." Jeff looked momentarily blank. And then he snapped his fingers. "Allison. Her name's Allison. Don't ask for a last. I have no idea."

Allison?

Drew's shoulders slumped. "Oh," he answered, unable to keep the disappointment from his voice.

Jeff laughed. "What? Don't you date women named Allison?"

Drew shrugged. "I'm not much into blind dates."

"Yeah," his brother-in-law lamented. "Don't blame you much there. I met Amanda on a blind date."

Drew lifted his face and frowned as the insult to his sister hit him all the way to the core. But Jeff was quick to add, "I mean, that's the only time I ever saw a set up actually work."

Calming, Drew took a quick drink. He studied his brother-in-law from the corner of his eye. From the very beginning, Jeff had liked to talk about women a little too much whenever he was away from his wife. From the stories he'd told Drew, he'd been the ultimate player before he'd gotten married.

But Mandy had never voiced a concern over his fidelity . . . until now. Drew had to think if Jeff had done something wrong, he hadn't only started doing it recently. Because, honestly, why would he wait all these years when he'd had a wandering eyes for the entire duration? It didn't make sense. Ergo, Mandy had to be wrong. No way would it take her twelve years to figure out something this big.

The interior of the house that sat on 410 South Elm had been silent for nearly twenty-four hours. Mia wasn't certain what to do about it. She hated being on the outs with her roommate. Piper had been there, by her side, through the worst part of her life.

But she didn't want her roommate to think she approved of Piper's scandalous activities either because, honestly, what was worse than dating a married man?

Mia shivered. She never would've guessed her friend could lower herself to such levels. Piper was so vivacious and energetic. Men flocked to her in droves. She could have her pick from any number of single men out there. Why would she —

"Mi Mi?"

Jumping, Mia spun from the kitchen counter where she'd been quietly slathering Miracle Whip on a piece of bread to make herself a sandwich and found Piper huddled in the doorway, her entire stance uncertain and hesitant, which totally wasn't the Piper she knew.

"Are you still mad at me?"

"Oh, Pipe." Mia's shoulders slumped. She sat down the butter knife. "I was never mad at you. I'm just really concerned. What you're doing is not only immoral, but dangerous. What if his wife is crazy enough to hurt you?"

After meeting Amanda Wright, Mia had

to think her anxiety wasn't too far-fetched either. There had been something lethal and unhinged in Mandy's glare when Mia had met her the day before.

"Well, you don't have to worry about it anymore," Piper said. She lowered her gaze and focused on her hands she had clasped against her stomach. "I . . . I broke up with him. Last night." When she lifted her face, she still looked guilty, biting her lip and staring at Mia as if she expected to receive ten lashes for her announcement.

Relief swarming through her, Mia let out a big grin. "You did? Piper, that's wonderful. And very smart."

Still appearing uncertain as she gifted Mia with a tremulous smile, Piper asked, "So . . . you're not mad at me anymore?"

"I was never mad at you," Mia repeated and even drifted forward to envelope Piper in a tight, but quick, hug. "But I'm much more proud of you now."

"Thank goodness." Piper sighed and squeezed Mia tight before letting go and pulling back. "I don't think I could stand it if you didn't like me anymore. You're my best friend, Mi Mi."

Touched that Piper felt so strongly about keeping their friendship alive, Mia reached out and covered her roommate's fingers with her own. "You're my best friend too. And don't worry about me deserting you. I'll always be here for you. No matter what."

Piper's smile was relieved; she once again looked like her confident self. "Thank you. That's exactly what I needed to hear."

Mandy attacked as soon as Drew slipped back into the kitchen.

"So . . . did you notice anything off?"

Drew sighed and pressed his back to the closed door. Jeff had decided to finish his third beer and had stayed behind in the garage.

"No," he said. "And to be honest, the only person acting strange today was you."

She sent him a questioning look. "But —"

He held up a hand. "I know you're going to hate me for saying this, but I don't think he's cheating on you." It was either that, or he'd never been faithful in the first place . . . something she hopefully would've figured out a long time ago.

"So, what about the flowers?"

"Ask him about them already," Drew ground out. "I'm sure he'll have a perfectly reasonable explanation."

"And what about the . . . the other?"

Drew winced and held up a hand as if that would block the words from reaching his ears. "Mandy, please. I just ate."

"I'm serious, Drew. Why hasn't he acted interested —"

"Once again, I think you need to talk to him about it. Not me." Please, God. Never Drew.

"I can't ask yet," she answered, pitching her voice low. "And you know why."

He sighed. "Look —"

But the door to the garage was opening and a blissfully unaware Jeff stepped into the kitchen to join them.

"I gotta go," Drew muttered, glancing once toward Jeff, and then turning and walking from the house. He didn't stop to say bye to his nieces and nephew as he usually did, but trotted straight to his truck, not pausing until he sat behind the wheel with the engine running. Then he glanced up at his sister's place. It was as nice and peaceful looking as any house. The perfect family home. Staring at it, Drew remembered another house, very similar to it, almost a replica of this one. From the outside, it had looked flawless and pristine. But inside, a mother paced, itching to leave her husband and two kids. Itching to leave Drew.

She'd waited until his first day of second grade before she'd skipped out on them and never returned. And the only person he'd had to rely on after that was Mandy, Mandy who'd been forced to raise him not as a big sister but more like a single parent. He wouldn't be anything today if it wasn't for her and her steady presence.

Guilt weighing on him, he geared his truck into reverse and backed out of her drive. His sister never asked him for help. And yet, here she was, needing one simple favor and he was failing her.

No, he didn't think Jeff was cheating, or at least that he'd taken up the habit recently, but that didn't mean he should brush the subject aside like he was.

Amanda needed answers, so he'd get them.

Five minutes later, he parked at the curb in front of 410 South Elm. He blew out a breath as he cut the engine. Yeah, he could do this. For Mandy, he could do this.

If he wanted to be perfectly honest, he wanted to do it for himself more. He needed to know what Mia's relationship with his brother-in-law entailed just as much as he needed to explore the intense chemistry that flowed between them.

Knocking on the front door of the light green bungalow, Drew wiped his suddenly damp palms on his jeans, wondering what in the world he was going to say to her.

An apology would be a good start. He and Amanda had scared her to death the day before.

When he heard footsteps inside, he braced for the punch of longing he'd experienced the other two times he'd seen Mia. Ready to start talking as soon as he saw her and apologizing profusely so she wouldn't slam the door in his face, Drew sucked in a breath.

But as the door opened, Mia's face didn't greet him. All the bunched tension inside him deflated.

Who was this?

With long hair, tinted about fifty different shades of blond and brown and red, the lithe figure that greeted him had him pulling back and frowning.

"Uh . . ." Stepping backward another foot, he read the address. When he saw the numbers 410, he turned reluctantly back to the woman. "Is . . . Mia here?"

The woman froze. Her gaze slid down his body and then a moment later, she sent him a blinding smile. "Oh," she breathed. "You must be Drew."

"I . . ." Huh? "Yeah. How did you —"

"Come in, come in," she told him, taking his arm and practically yanking him into the front parlor. He stumbled across the threshold and into a tidy living room, decorated in tones of blue.

"Mi Mi!" The woman called, turning away from him to cup her hands around her mouth. "You have a visitor." She instantly whirled back and flashed him a wide smile. "She'll be right here," she murmured and couldn't seem to stop staring or smiling with a freaky, knowing glint in her eyes.

He cleared his throat and had to glance away, way too uncomfortable under such extreme inspection. But the woman wouldn't stop gawking.

He treated her to a tense smile. "So, ah . . . Not to be rude or anything. But, uh, how do you know my name?"

"Whoops." She threw back her head and barked out a quick laugh even as she reached out to touch his shoulder. "Sorry about that. I'm Piper Holliday. Mia's room-mate."

He drew back in surprise. "Oh." *Oh.*
Oh, no.

"She's mentioned you," Piper added and gave him a huge, stunning grin.

His stomach knotted painfully.

"Really?" he couldn't help but ask, hoping he didn't sound as hopeful as he felt.

He wasn't sure what surprised him more.

The fact that Mia had a roommate or that she'd mentioned him to said roommate.

"Piper, what's —"

Mia appeared in the arched opening of the room and slowed to a shocked halt.

His pulse beat a hard tattoo through his body. Shoving his hands into his pockets, he breathed out the word, "Hi."

She closed her mouth. "Drew? What're you doing here?" Her gaze zipped from her roommate to him and then back to her roommate before settling on him.

"Uh . . ." he glanced toward Piper. No way could he apologize in front of her roommate — her roommate, who also lived at 410 South Elm.

"You know," Piper broke the loud silence and started to back toward the exit. "I was just about to head to the mall. So, if you two will excuse me." She paused to scoop up a purse and a set of keys by the door.

"Drew," she added. "It was nice to meet you."

He swallowed. "Yeah." He wasn't certain if it was so nice, though. Sure, it seemed to clear Mia from guilt. But it didn't clear Jeff . . . at all.

Neither he nor Mia spoke until they heard Piper's car start outside and back down her drive.

Then he lifted his face. "You have a room-mate."

Mia's lips compressed in a tight line. "What are you doing here, Drew?" Her voice was in no way welcoming.

He blew out a breath and started to lift his hands to sift his fingers through his hair. But that's when he caught sight of the flowers.

"Oh, man," he whispered.

Mia followed his stare and immediately stepped into his line of vision, though they both knew the damage had already been done.

Betrayed, he sent her look.

"You didn't get a delivery of flowers, huh?" he murmured, moving toward them.

"Drew —" she started.

But he ignored her. "I guess that means these are for your roommate then. For Piper."

And yes, there was the note, sticking up between the buds, with the word "Piper" stenciled out in a man's heavy scrawl. Was it Jeff's writing? He had no idea.

He reached for the envelope, but Mia caught his arm.

"You can't read her note."

Meeting her gaze, he said, "I'm sorry," and tugged free of her grip. Snagging it, he tore the card from the envelope and scanned the message.

It read, *Thinking of you. J.*

Peeking around his elbow, Mia let out a breath of sound as she read the note as well. But he couldn't tell if it was from relief or disappointment.

"This doesn't mean anything," she said, sounding defensive. "A lot of people have names that start with J."

He turned. "What? Don't you know what J stands for? Didn't your roommate tell you who sent her the flowers?" She didn't answer; Drew clenched his teeth. "Don't you even care that she might be destroying a marriage? A family. This isn't just my sister's happiness at stake. She and Jeff have three kids together."

"Please, don't," Mia whispered. Her eyes looked tortured.

He took her arm and tried to coax her closer but she resisted. "Just tell me you didn't know."

She lifted her chin, looking defiant and scared at the same time. "I think you need to leave."

He dropped her arm. "Why?"

"I asked you not to open that card, Drew."

He snorted out a sound of disbelief. "You can't blame me for wanting to know the truth. For needing to know the truth."

"No, but I can blame you for not respecting my wishes."

"Mia, this is my sister's —"

"And Piper's my best friend," she cried. "I won't tell you what I do or don't know about her private life."

"I don't care about Piper. Just tell me if you knew or not."

"What does it matter? They're not my secrets to reveal."

"I have to know."

She glanced away. "Will you please just go?"

He blew out a frustrated groan. It killed him that she stood so close, smelling so good, and yet he was unable to convey the emotions roiling through him. He just wanted to reach out and yank her against him.

As the image only grew in his head, he shivered. What the heck. He was already batting zero here. What was one more strike from a woman he probably wouldn't see again?

"Mia, you're right. It doesn't matter. I can't be upset with you for being a good friend and keeping your roommate's confidence."

She lifted her face, looking cautious and

wary by his sudden change in attitude.

"I just . . ." He blew out some of the steam building in him. "I'm actually relieved. I didn't want it to be you. From the first moment I saw you, I felt . . ." He shook his head, the sensation stronger than before, swelling in his chest.

Her eyes widened and lips parted.

"I don't know how to describe it," he finished. "But it happened again yesterday. And it's happening right now. I can't just ignore this."

She took a jerking step back. "Maybe you should try harder."

Despite the uneasy way she eyed him, he grinned. "You feel it too, don't you?"

"No," she was quick to reply, unable to keep eye contact as the statement blurted from her.

His lips spread. "Liar."

Scorching an indignant glare his way, her back stiffened. "You need to leave. Right now."

"Don't be afraid, Mia." He kept his voice soft and his gaze kind, though he couldn't stop himself from reaching out to wrap a long lock of her pale hair around his finger. When she gave a light gasp but didn't yank away, he murmured, "I'm just as unsettled by this pull as you are."

Her eyes lifted, still apprehensive but also hopeful. "You don't look unsettled."

He smiled, ecstatic she'd stopped fighting the truth. "Here," he told her, dropping her hair to catch her hand and press it against his racing heart. "That's not what a settled person's heart feels like, is it?"

Her gaze fell to her fingers as they lay spread against his chest. Her breathing grew stuttered, almost as if her anxiety was about to make her hyperventilate. But she continued to press her palm to him.

She lifted her face, looking extremely panicked. "I don't . . . I can't . . ."

"Shh," he said and covered her hand with his own so he was able to feel his own heartbeat thump through her shaking fingers. "It's okay."

Then he bent his head and brushed his mouth against hers.

CHAPTER SIX

Mia swayed forward, closing her eyes on instinct, and sank into Drew.

He had incredibly soft lips. Relaxed and soothed, she drifted, floating off the floor. It was a nice sensation. Alive and exhilarating. Drew didn't demand, but coaxed, tempting her to give more.

He tasted faintly of . . . beer.

She pulled back. "You have to go," she gasped and covered her betraying lips with trembling fingers.

For a moment, he merely swayed, his eyes still unfocused and hooded. Then his brow wrinkled, and he blinked. He stepped forward. "Mia —" He reached for her but she put up a hand, tears welling.

Her control shattering, she held fast onto the last few threads of composure. "You shouldn't have read that note," she whispered, shaking her head furiously.

He froze. "But —"

"If you thought I'd betray my best friend to you over a kiss, you're delusional."

"What?" His mouth fell open, and shock rose, evident on his face.

She shook her head. "Just leave me alone."

Spinning away, she ran all the way to her room, slamming the door and throwing herself on her bed.

He was still in the house. His presence overwhelmed her like a barbell pinned to her chest. But he didn't stay long. Her ears strained as she listened to the soft tread of his shoes fade and then the front door squeak open and then close again. Finally, the pressure on her lungs eased and she sucked in air.

Her face burned from the strength of her tears and she buried her scorching cheeks into a cool pillow. Wrapping her arms around the cushion, she squeezed her wet lashes together and tried to imagine herself somewhere else. Her happy place.

It was a technique Dr. Higgins had taught her.

Escape.

Man, she was pathetic.

Yelling at him for reading Piper's note had really only been an excuse. In truth, she'd been petrified. For three years, she'd struggled to feel real again. But here, the first moment it began to actually happen, she ran away like a little baby. Like a coward. Drew had been her first kiss since Ryan.

Drew slapped the palm of his hand against the steering wheel. He scowled at the front door of Mia's house and contemplated getting out and going back inside. He wanted to know what had gone wrong . . . what he'd done wrong. That kiss had just been starting to get good and then, wow, she'd burst into tears on him.

Confused and frustrated because he had no idea what had gone awry, he continued to sit there, scrutinizing her house until his phone rang. He groaned, not ready to talk to Mandy at all. Digging the cell out of his pocket to cut the ring, he glanced at the caller ID, only to discover it wasn't his sister after all.

It was worse.

His father.

He swallowed, wondering when he'd last talked to the old man. Hmm. It'd been . . . Christmas? Yes, Christmas. Mandy had badgered him into going with her and her kids to their father's on Christmas Eve.

Blowing out a breath, he flipped the phone open and pressed it to his ear for a good three seconds.

"Hello," he finally said.

"Hey . . . Drew?" the almost unfamiliar voice of Don Harper spoke. He sounded confident enough with the "hey," but by the time he added Drew's name, he lacked conviction. "This is your dad."

Drew wanted to snort. He'd figured that fact out. The million-dollar question was why his father suddenly deemed Drew important enough to contact.

"Yeah," he answered. "What did you need?"

"Oh." Out of breath, his dad said, "I . . . well . . . as you know, Evie's going to be a senior next year."

No, actually Drew had no idea. He didn't keep tabs on his stepsiblings. "Okay," he murmured, wondering what the heck his dad was getting at.

"So, we — I, actually — was wondering if you could take her senior picture."

Blood thundered through Drew's ears. He tried to quell the instant spurt of irritation and, yes, jealousy but managed to tap it down. Still . . . his dad sure hadn't hired any professional photographer to take his or Mandy's senior picture when they'd been in school.

"Um. Sure," he said. "I guess. Yeah, that's fine."

Wondering if his dad was asking for a freebie or what, he hesitated before saying, "When do you . . ." Coming up with a void, he tipped his head up and stared at the front door of 410 S. Elm. A picture filled his head of Mia the first moment she'd turned and looked up him with her innocent watering can in hand.

Tranquility filled him.

Shaking his head, he blinked and returned to reality, wondering what in the world had just happened there. Odd. Definitely odd. But for some reason, his mind felt less muddled now. And realizing he was stuttering around for no reason, he took another breath.

He shot senior pictures all the time. All he had to do was treat this like any other client.

"Okay," he said, falling into business mode. "Well, first we need to set up a clothing consultation, so I can decide which backdrops will match her outfits."

"Oh. Yeah, about that . . ." His dad broke in. "I was hoping she could take them here . . . at our house. Candace wants a picture of her in the gazebo."

An uncomfortable chill raced up the back

of Drew's neck. He pictured the house he'd grown up in. The gazebo hadn't been there during his stay. His dad had built it for his second wife, Candace, as a wedding present.

Drew knew he couldn't fault his father for remarrying. Don had been considerate enough to wait until Drew had left for college before moving in his new family. Still, it felt incredibly odd seeing his dad with "them" and knowing they were more important to him than Drew or Mandy had ever been.

"Drew?" his dad's voice echoed through his ear. "You still there?"

"Yeah," he answered. "That's fine. Pictures at your place sound great. I can bring a backdrop with me too if she wants a more traditional look for her yearbook."

"That would be wonderful," his father said, sounding relieved. "So when would be a good time for you?"

After deciding to meet the next Saturday, there was a pause. Then Don Harper added, "And Candace thought since you'd be over anyway, you, ah, might . . . She'd like a family picture of the five of us together."

Drew swallowed.

The five of them. That would be his father, Candace, her two kids — Evie and Jack — and Brianna, Drew's half sister. No room for a Drew or Mandy in that count. He had to wonder if there'd ever been room for him in his father's life.

"That's fine," he managed to murmur.

"Good." His father blew out a relieved breath. "Good. I'll see you Saturday then."

"See you Saturday," Drew echoed as he disconnected. He closed his eyes and pressed the phone to his forehead. "What next?" he muttered.

In answer, his phone chimed again. He fell back in his seat and glanced at Mia's house, remembering how nice her mouth had been. And when her body had pressed into his —

He shivered and answered the phone, wondering what his dad wanted him to take a picture of now. "Hello."

"I was wrong," Mandy said in his ear. "Jeffrey's not cheating on me."

He closed his eyes. So not the person he wanted to talk to. But the determined tone in her voice had him sitting up.

"You talked to him?" It was about time.

"Yes."

Drew exhaled a long, pent up breath. *Oh, thank you.* His suspicions about Mia's roommate were wrong. Jeff wasn't a cheating jerk and life could return to normal. "What's the deal with the flowers then?"

109

His sister paused.

He frowned. "Mandy?"

"I . . . I didn't ask."

"You didn't — Amanda!"

He gritted his teeth and reached forward to turn on the ignition. As the truck's engine hummed under him, he sent one last regretful look toward the front door and pulled away from the curb.

"I thought about what you said. He didn't act weird around you. And he's having a lot of stress. I'm going to just . . . let it go at that. Yeah . . . I'm just going to believe him."

"Well . . . Good." Though, good was very opposite of what he meant.

Mandy didn't sound at all like she believed Jeff was innocent. Frowning, he reached the end of the block, braked at the intersection and waited for a truck to pass. All the while, his gut twisted into knots.

He had more ammunition for her and she was giving up on her quest. Not sure what to do, he listened to her depressed tone as she said, "So . . . just forget I ever said anything. Okay. Please don't mention this to Jeffrey . . . or tell him about how I tried to confront his mistress. Okay?"

He clenched his fingers around the steering wheel. "Ah . . . okay."

"Thanks, Drew. You're the best." She

started to hang up. And he almost let her go.

Just let it be, his mind warned him, even as he rushed out the words, "Mandy, wait."

There was a pause. He told himself if she'd already hung up, he'd let it go.

But she said, "Yeah?"

He swallowed, still deliberating. Should he tell her? He pondered briefly, then turned into a gas station and muttered, "Will you go to Dad's with me next Saturday? He just called and wants me to take Evie's senior picture."

He closed his eyes briefly, disappointed with himself for being such a coward. Since the first winter break of his freshman year at college when he'd come home to find his room taken over by his six-year-old stepbrother, Jack, Drew hadn't been comfortable with his father. Or maybe it had started before that. They'd never been close since his dad had never been home. He just hadn't realized the lack of affection until he'd seen the man give Candace's children so much of it.

"Of course I'll come," Mandy sounded insulted he even had to ask. She'd always been there for him, even that first semester break when he'd had nowhere to go. She might've been a newlywed and pregnant with her first baby, but she and Jeff had made room for him in their home, and there he'd felt wanted.

"Thanks," he said.

Now if only he'd give her the support she'd always given him. Gritting his teeth, he blurted out, "She has a roommate."

"What?" Mandy said.

"Mia," he mumbled, telling himself to shut up already. Let Mandy think what she wanted to think. "She has a roommate." He parked in front of a pump and squeezed his eyes closed, calling himself every kind of idiot for stirring the pot.

Silence reigned over the satellite connection. Then, "Excuse me?"

He could actually picture the frozen horror on his sister's face. Man, what did he think he was doing? She was ready to move past this, and he'd just bulldozed right over that idea.

"Tell me everything," she demanded.

He swallowed convulsively. It was too late to shut his trap now. The barn door was swinging wide open; the cows were wandering everywhere.

"I went over to her place today," he confessed. "To, you know, talk to her." Because he couldn't stay away. "And . . . and her roommate answered the door."

"Roommate?" Mandy repeated breathlessly. "Are . . . are you sure it was a roommate, not just some friend visiting."

"They introduced her to me as a roommate. Her name's Piper. Piper Holliday."

"Piper," Mandy whispered the name.

He gave a silent nod. "She . . ."

"She what?" Mandy prodded impatiently.

Drew hesitated. "She seems more like the type to, you know."

"Cheat?" Mandy guessed.

After a sigh, he murmured, "Yeah." He knew exactly what he was doing, deflecting speculation away from Mia. And in the process, he was once again opening his sister's uncertainty. "Look," he started. "Just ignore me. Forget I said anything. I didn't mean to —"

"No, it's okay," his sister assured. "I've already forgotten it."

He nodded though he knew she was lying. "Good."

"Good," she repeated way too brightly. "I'll see you later. Bye."

She hung up before he could stop her. Slowly, Drew slid from his truck to pump gas, all the while berating himself for upsetting Mandy.

"Have you thought about what we discussed

last week?"

Mia gave a brief nod, keeping her hands fisted in her lap.

Dr. Higgins eyed her over the top of his bifocals. "And? Are you ready to try?"

No way. "Okay," she murmured. "We can give it a try."

He smiled, pleased like some adoring old grandfather, completely blissful to any problems. "And have you been keeping up with your journal?"

"Yes," she lied.

He nodding, approving. "Good." Folding his hands, he leaned forward, resting his elbows on the surface of his desk. "Now . . . What is your biggest fear about letting go?"

Mia swallowed. Geez. They were going to address it already? What happened to small talk about the weather first? It was really cloudy out today. A strong chance of rain. Didn't he think it was going to rain?

Giving a half-hearted shrug, she mumbled, "I don't know."

"Are you afraid of being happy?"

She couldn't meet his probing stare. "I don't know." Yes, she was terrified of happiness. What if someone else died while she smiled, blissfully unaware her life was about to fall apart? What if she laughed and —

Dr. Higgins sighed. "Mia . . ."

Her breathing escalated; she turned to stare out the window. His frustration filled the room with that single sigh. But he couldn't be any more bothered than she was about all this. It occupied her every thought, crowded her sleep and intruded into each corner of her life. She'd nearly completed her five-step process over healing.

She couldn't help but wonder, though, what happened after the final phase, once she accepted reality and finished the steps? Did she graduate, get a good-job sticker pasted to her shirt, a pat on the back? You're healed. Now go forth and . . . what? She had no idea. So, she stuck with the steps, clung to them desperately. She didn't like being this close to the end.

Her life had become steps and stages and she wasn't sure if she could live without them. It was so much safer this way. It was her haven. Her badge of existence.

If someone started to worry or pry too deeply, she could always pull her handy badge and flash it their way. It's okay. I'm in grief counseling, working my way through the steps. And like magic, they always nodded and backed off. Like they understood.

Dr. Higgins was starting to see through the ruse though. He'd cracked his way inside her head and he knew; she was stalling.

"I know I've suggested group counseling before and you didn't feel ready but . . ."

She shook her head in an adamant gesture.

"I was hoping you'd become more adjusted to the idea," he finished, his shoulders falling as he watched the panicked look cross her face.

But group counseling? Had he lost his mind? She'd barely grown comfortable talking to one person — him — about the pain. No way could she spell it out to an entire room full of people. Then she'd have to sit there and listen to their stories in return. No, thank you. It was hard enough to shoulder her own misery. No way could she handle someone else's too.

"Breathe, Mia."

Dr. Higgins' voice floated through her and she unconsciously opened her lungs, sucking in air. Her pulse beat against the sides of her neck, and she pressed her hand to the front of her throat like that could actually stop the pounding.

"Gooooood," the counselor cooed. "Close your eyes and concentrate on breathing. One breath in. And one breath out." She obeyed, shutting out his office and staring at the insides of her eyelids, focusing on working her lungs. In and out.

"Go to your happy place, Mia. Relax for a minute."

She nodded, letting him know she heard his suggestion. But when she forced her mind to envision the beach full of white sand and bright blue waters she usually pictured, she glanced over to the beach chair next to hers and found Drew Harper in a pair of swimming trunks. His eyes remained hidden behind a pair of black shades as he sipped from a tall glass with an umbrella toothpick holding together a cherry and a chunk of pineapple.

After swallowing, he sighed, refreshed and sat the drink aside. Then he turned to her, white teeth glistening as he smiled. "The bartender sure knows how to mix a drink," he murmured, leaning over the arm of his chair to move closer toward her.

"But it still doesn't taste as good as you." He continued to smile as he pressed his mouth to hers.

Mia held her breath, waiting for the moist, softness of his lips. For his taste. But when it never came, she remembered this was only happening in her mind.

Her eyes flew open; a sob caught in her throat.

What in the world?

How had Drew Harper invaded her happy place? He didn't belong there. She only went there for peace and quiet. For sanctuary. Not to experience some hanky-panky with the deceiving photographer.

She hadn't desired a man since Lexie was alive and Ryan was still in her life. It felt wrong to experience longing now. And actually like the sensation.

When she realized her cheeks were wet, she sniffed and glanced guiltily toward Dr. Higgins. "I'm sorry," she whispered.

He shook his head. "There's no need for apologies. No one here's going to get upset if you fail. You tried. That's what is important."

She nodded, but inside the disappointment sliced through her. She wiped at her tears and told herself she would stop thinking about Drew Harper if it was the last thing she did.

CHAPTER SEVEN

"Thanks again for coming with me." Drew slung the strap of his camera bag over his shoulder and glanced at Mandy. There were purple smudges under her eyes, and he knew his call last Sunday was the reason for any lack of sleep she'd experienced. He should've kept his big trap shut.

He wanted to apologize and somehow make it up to her, but this was definitely not the time or place. He had to get through the next couple of hours first.

Behind him, his two nieces and one nephew piled out of the backseat of Mandy's car he'd been driving and raced toward the entrance of his childhood home. As they sprinted, they all yelled, "Brianna!"

In answer, the front door swung open and his seven-year-old half sister streaked outside, waving to Natalie, Lucy, and Felix. He watched their reunion as the four danced in circles and jabbered a hundred miles an hour in kid talk. His little sister, Brianna, was definitely a happy child. But then, twenty-two years his junior, she'd never experienced any of the childhood he or Mandy had. And she had a different mother as well as a father who no longer worked eighty hours a week to pay the bills.

She had dark, curly hair exactly like his, which always made his stomach hurt when he saw her. This girl was blood of his blood and he felt as removed from her as he did Candace's other two children.

Next to him, Mandy said, "I think I would've been in trouble if we hadn't come with you." There was amusement in her voice as she watched the children. "They love visiting Bri."

Delighted to see her smile, Drew's breathing became easier. "Don't leave me," he said under this breath. "You're my assistant today."

She rolled her eyes. "Why're you always so afraid to come to Dad's alone?"

"I'm not afraid," he muttered, sending her a moody frown.

He was uncomfortable. After living here for eighteen years, he'd become a visitor the moment his father and Candace had moved her son, Jack, into his room.

"But you can stay in the guest room,

Drew," Candace assured.

Shaking his head, Drew forced a smile. "That's okay. Don't worry about it. I'll . . . find somewhere else." The shock was still rolling through him, making his insides numb. But he couldn't believe it. His dad had given his room away.

"Are you sure?" his dad asked. "We'd love to have you."

Again, Drew shook his head. We'd love to have you? You fed that polite nonsense to a stranger. Not family.

It told him exactly how much he didn't fit into his dad's life.

"Well, you look terrified out of your mind," Amanda teased, jostling him in the arm with her elbow.

He glanced at her soberly, picturing her ten years younger, leading him into her spare bedroom. He'd followed hesitantly, like an intruder in his sister's home.

"Are you sure it's okay if I sleep here?" he asked.

She sent him a puzzled, annoyed look. "Don't be stupid. Of course, you can stay here any time you like. You're my brother."

He nodded, not answering, and scanned his new room. Amanda had decorated it in pastels with angel posters on the wall.

"I can understand why you don't want to

121

bother Dad since he's a newlywed and everything."

Forcing another nod, Drew stepped toward his new bed and set his duffle bag on the mattress.

"So, what do you think of Candace?" Amanda asked behind him. "She seems really nice, doesn't she?"

He turned slowly and examined Amanda's face. She looked truly happy for their dad. Not wanting to show his hurt feelings, he agreed. "Yeah . . . She's nice."

But why hadn't his dad invited him to their wedding? Why hadn't he even bothered to introduce her to his son first?

Mandy hugged him. "I'm glad he finally found someone."

Drew could only keep nodding in agreement, totally alone in his irrational envy and heartache.

"I'm not scared," he repeated to his sister now. "Just nervous. I want to do a good job on Evie's pictures."

As if realizing this was the perfect time for her entrance, his seventeen-year-old stepsister hurried from the house, charging straight toward them.

"Drew!" she exclaimed, throwing herself at him and hugging him heartily. "You're here."

Having never been hugged by her before, he lifted his arms in surprise. "Uh . . . yeah."

"She's not excited or anything," his father's voice told him.

Drew lifted his face to find Don Harper smiling at his stepdaughter. Returning the grin, Drew murmured, "I can tell."

As Evie pulled away from him, Don tugged her close to his side and wrapped a companionable arm around her shoulder. "You sure you're ready for this?" he asked Drew.

Drew patted the camera bag resting on his hip. "I guess so."

"Let's start in the gazebo," Evie said, already pulling away from Don and hurrying around the back of the house.

Helpless to follow her order, the three adults followed. All the while, Drew made sure his sister stuck close.

By six o'clock that evening, all the pictures had been taken, yet Drew found himself still standing in his father's backyard, holding a Styrofoam plate smeared with leftover traces of a grilled hamburger and potato salad. He still wasn't sure how his father's wife had talked them into staying for a cookout, but here he stood, still plastered close to Mandy's side.

"Now that we've finally found a private moment," she murmured, stepping close to speak in a conspiratorially low voice.

They stood on the opposite side of the yard as her and Candace's children, who were playing tag. Don and Candace had just carried leftovers inside.

"She's a hair stylist," Amanda said, not looking at Drew as she spoke but keeping her eyes on Natalie, Lucy, and Felix.

He blinked, totally confused. "What? Who is?"

"Piper Holliday." Her lip curled with contempt as the name hissed its way from her lips. "I googled her. She works at Styles R Us." Her blue eyes turbulent like the ocean just before a hurricane, she added, "That's where Jeffrey gets his hair cut."

Drew swallowed, trying to focus. But at the mention of Mia's roommate, her face popped into his mind. He'd be old and gray before he forgot the first moment she turned from watering her flowers and met his gaze. His heart palpitated just thinking about it.

But, no, they weren't talking about Mia. The roommate, he reminded himself. Focus on the roommate.

"She cuts his hair?" he asked his sister.

Amanda bit her lip. "I don't think so. His

hairdresser's name is Darla. But at least this explains how they met."

He nodded and didn't plan on asking, "Does Mia work there too?" but the words spilled from his mouth before he could check them.

His sister nailed him with a perturbed look, her eyes narrowed and lips pressed flat with disapproval. "How should I know? I don't care about her."

He cleared his throat and glanced away. "So . . . what? You didn't google Mia when you thought she was dating Jeff."

Sighing as if his question was the stupidest thing she'd ever been asked, Amanda said, "I didn't know Mia's last name."

Right. Come to think of it, he didn't know Mia's last name either.

"I didn't discover much else about her," Amanda continued, returning to the Piper subject. "But I found some newspaper article online about her graduating high school eight years ago."

That would make her what . . . twenty-six, twenty-seven. He wondered if she was the same age as Mia. Mia certainly looked younger. She had such a fresh, smooth face. But there'd been something ancient in her eyes, like something had prematurely aged her. He wondered what could've been so

125

awful as to wear her down like that.

"Think you can coax any information out of the roommate. Out of this Mia woman," Amanda said. "Since you're so in love with her."

He lifted his face at the mention of Mia. "Mandy," he started.

"You can act interested in her while spying on her worthless roommate."

He frowned. Act interested? There would be no acting involved.

"She'd probably go out with you," Mandy continued. "I mean, she came to your house to give you addresses for houses for sale. That right there says she's interested."

"You think?" he couldn't help but ask. His sister scowled at the hopeful note in his voice. He cleared his throat, needing to redirect the attention from Mia. "You know what. I'm not doing it. You need to talk to your husband, Mandy. I refuse to use Mia like that."

She opened her mouth to comment, but a female voice called from behind him. "What're you two gossiping about over here by yourselves?"

Drew looked up to find both Candace and his father approaching. Candace smiled — as she usually did. His dad didn't look so pleased. But he was the type that would follow his second wife into the grave if he had to . . . which, by the expression on his face, looked to be the case.

"Mind if we join you?" Candace asked.

"Not at all," Amanda answered, making Drew question which woman perfected the cheerful act better.

It made him wonder how many times his sister had grinned at him, when in fact she was probably sobbing inside. He studied her while she and Candace exchanged pleasantries, talking about motherhood. She didn't look at all like the woman he'd been talking to thirty seconds earlier, like she might burst into tears any moment.

"So, Drew . . ." His father sidled up to him and shoved his hands into his pockets, jingling the change inside. "Evie seems real pleased with her poses."

Drew had to fight to keep from rolling his eyes. He doubted his father could've come up with a lamer topic to discuss. "We'll have to wait 'til the proofs are done before knowing if she's going to like them or not," he answered. It was probably a rude thing to say, but he'd been unable to stop himself.

"Oh, I'm sure she'll love them," Candace spoke up, dropping her conversation with Amanda to break into the men's discussion to keep the tone polite, no doubt.

"You have no idea how grateful we are to you, Drew. Evie's been talking about nothing else but getting these pictures all year."

Drew forced a smile, thinking they shouldn't have to be grateful. He was family. Taking all the pictures around here should've been expected of him. But, no, everyone was so polite and so frustratingly distant.

"Felix!" Amanda yelled from beside him, making him jump. "Stop hitting Jack."

The six youngsters continued to play tag across the yard as if they hadn't heard her. Down from Evie at seventeen to Felix at four, they all laughed and darted away from Lucy who was obviously "it."

"Oh, they're fine. They get along so well together," Candace said, sounding pleased. When she turned back, she paused dramatically to stare between Mandy and Don. "You know, I think it's amazing the similarities between you and your dad, Amanda."

Drew frowned and eyed his stepmother. Just what kind of similarities was she talking about? Drew was the one who'd ended up looking like a replica of his father.

But then Candace continued. "You both have two girls and a boy. Natalie, Lucy, and Felix pair off so nicely with Evie, Jack, and Bri."

Jaw dropping, Drew glanced toward Amanda. She gave a slight shake of her head, warning him to keep his mouth shut. But the indignation burned its way down his throat and he ached to say something.

Candace never purposely left him and Amanda out of the family, but it was always the little things she did that let him know he was an outsider. Without fail, she always forgot to set him a place when Amanda drug him along for Christmas. And now . . . saying Don Harper only had three children . . . Evie, Jack, and Brianna. Guess that left Drew an orphan now. Abandoned by his mother and thrown over by his father for some other woman's kids.

His dad must've sensed the tension rolling off Drew, because he completely changed the subject, glancing at Amanda and asking, "How's Jeff doing these days?"

Amanda and Drew exchanged a quick look. He half hoped she'd open up and confess her suspicions. His dad would understand all about having a faithless spouse. Drew couldn't remember how many times his mother had cheated before she'd finally run off with some used car salesman.

But Amanda kept her problems to herself and smiled graciously. "He's just fine. Been going on a lot of business trips lately. But I say that's a good thing. Must mean a promotion is coming up."

As Candace and Don chuckled, Drew met Mandy's gaze. Jeff had been gone a lot? Why had he not known this? Guilt smacked him across the face. How long had his sister held suspicions about her husband's faithfulness? How long had she kept it inside without anyone else knowing? And would she still be keeping it all in now if Drew hadn't caught her marching from her house with a gun?

"We should probably be going soon," Amanda said, stepping closer to him.

He lifted his face, wondering how long he'd been spacing out and how much of the conversation he'd missed.

"Well, we're glad to spend so much time with you today," Candace said. She patted his shoulder. "And Drew. We can't thank you enough for Evie's pictures."

He nodded, once again the outsider. "No problem."

As his dad took Candace's hand and called a goodbye to his three grandchildren, Drew caught Amanda's arm and drew her to the side. She looked up at him in surprise.

There was nothing like a fresh reminder why he was so grateful to her.

"Okay," he relented. "I'll talk to Mia and

see what I can find out from her. Just . . .
give me a few days to decide how I'm going
to do this. All right?"

The nightmare that struck came to her in
wicked Technicolor. It was so vivid, she
could still smell Ryan's aftershave as he
tried to push her away.

"Ryan." She clutched his arm desperately.
"Please don't do this. Don't go. You have to
be strong for me."

But he only worked more vigorously to
pry her off him. She didn't like the clingy
Mia much either, but she didn't care about
how pathetic she must look. She needed his
support.

Finally shrugging her away, he stepped
back and shook his head. "And who's going
to be strong for me, Mia?" he wanted to
know. "I lost a child too."

She gasped, sitting straight up in bed.
Sweat had matted the back of her hair to
her neck. She shuddered out a trembling
breath and lifted her hand to her neck to
feel her erratic pulse. Shaking her head, she
shoved away the covers and stumbled off
the mattress to hurry into her bathroom.
Once the light was on and she started the
faucet, she lifted her face to the vanity mirror. Large grey eyes stared back, looking

frightened and alone.

"You're so pathetic," she told the image, cupping her hand under the stream and splashing water onto her cheeks.

Once she'd dried her face and changed into something that wasn't drenched in sweat, she crawled back between her warm sheets and closed her eyes. Wanting to see anything on the insides of her eyelids besides Ryan shoving her away, she concentrated on breathing. One breath in and one breath out.

Avoiding the beach scene, she focused on her past, looking for a happy memory instead. Lexie's face appeared in her head and she smiled instantly. But as soon as the precious little girl giggled her precious little baby laugh, awful memories followed and she sobbed out a moan.

It wasn't fair. She should be able to recall her baby without bawling. She wanted those happy memories back. She needed them like she needed air.

But it wasn't to be. Unconcerned about the guilt that would no doubt follow, she pictured Drew instead. Back in swimming trunks, he set his pale mixed drink aside and leaned toward her once again. She smiled, latching onto the image. He had such kind eyes, a safe and protective smile.

She could languish in his company and never once fear anything. He seemed like the easy-going type that wouldn't mind a clinger if something awful happened. He'd cuddle her, and unlike Ryan, would give any kind of support she craved.

He'd probably be a good daddy too. She remembered how he'd touched that baby's head in his studio. So caring and gentle. A reflection of Lexie wavered through her consciousness, learning to walk from Mia's arms. She imagined Drew catching her after three wobbly steps. He scooped her up into his arms and kissed her face until his beard stubble tickled her and made her wrinkle her nose.

Holding her close, he glanced toward Mia, and they shared a smile. "She's growing so fast."

Mia nodded. "Pretty soon, she'll be taking her first step down the wedding aisle."

Pulling Lexie close, Drew frowned and kissed her baby-fine hair. "No way. Not my little girl. I'm the only man for her. Right, Princess?"

Mia fell unconscious to that scene. Drew, who'd never even met her daughter, twirled Lexie — who'd never lived long enough to even take one step — in a circle. When he lifted Dream-Lexie up high, she screamed with giggles, begging him for more. Drifting into deep REM, Mia slept with a smile.

CHAPTER EIGHT

Mia sat at her computer, in her bedroom, shopping eBay for Piper's birthday. She'd just placed her bid for a Louis Vuitton purse her roommate would die for when the doorbell rang. Clicking on confirm bid, she clicked back into another screen to see if she was high bidder.

"No," she muttered, digging her teeth into her bottom lip.

The doorbell chimed again before she remembered Piper was gone, working out at the gym this afternoon. Brushing her fingers over her mouth and down the front of her shirt to ensure there was no more evidence left of the Oreos she'd delved into half an hour earlier, she stood and hurried to the entrance.

She pulled the main door open before checking who'd come to visit. And suddenly, there stood Drew, waiting on the other side of her screen door, hands shoved deep into his pockets and facing the street as he watched a handful of children purchase ice cream from a traveling vendor.

He turned when she opened the door. Their gazes met and caught; she forgot to breathe.

"Hi," he said, sounding a little oxygen-deprived.

Not sure how to react, she stood there. A million responses burst through her. She could slam the door in his face, tell him he was a lying jerk . . . or she could open the screen and pull him into a grateful hug.

It felt so good to see him again. After dreaming about him with Lexie, he looked exactly like the vision she'd created. Even his smile was the same . . . though he hadn't had that uncertain, apologetic look in his eyes last night when he'd pulled Lexie into his arms.

"You probably don't believe me," he started. "But I actually came over here last time to apologize for the scene at my studio. But now that I think of it, I never did tell you how sorry I was, did I?" He winced and finished, "I only upset you more."

Mia didn't answer. She merely stared at him.

He shifted weight from foot to foot. "Do you want me to apologize out here?" When she still refused to respond, he nodded and sent her a stiff smile. "Okay," he said. "That's fine."

He blew out a breath and glanced up at the sky as if silently scanning his brain, trying to remember what he'd rehearsed to say. "Okay," he repeated. "I am sincerely sorry for misleading you the first time we met. I hope you realize I didn't mean it for spite. Never for that. I did have a reason. And I never, ever meant to deceive or hurt you."

"I'm not hurt." She folded her arms over her chest to rub at her suddenly chilled arms.

No, she wasn't hurt. She was devastated.

"Oh." He looked at her askance as if he didn't believe her, but he didn't call her on it. Instead, he sucked in a breath and said, "Good. That's good. I'd also like to apologize for disrespecting your wishes and reading the card that came with the roses."

He paused, giving her a chance to respond. She lifted an eyebrow, letting him know she needed more groveling. His lips tightened, repressing his amusement.

Glancing away, he continued. "I know you're mad. But I did what I felt I had to do."

At her sharp frown, he quickly explained, "Mandy's more than just a sister to me. See, my mom left when I was little. But it didn't really faze me because . . . well, there was always Amanda. My sister pretty much raised me. She stepped into the slot of mother without even blinking, even though she was still in high school. I remember she had to quit the volleyball team so she could stay home with me every night."

Not sure if he was feeding her some sob story — whether it was the truth or a lie — to gain her sympathies so he could sneak some Piper information from her, she studied him a moment before curiosity caught the better of her.

"What about your dad? Where was he?"

He glanced down at his shoes. "He had to find a second job. We rarely saw him. Amanda was the one that kept our family together. I know it had to be hard for her. I certainly never made it any easier. I was a typical kid, always managing to get myself into trouble."

"I wonder why I believe that part of your story?" she murmured.

He grinned, and she bit the inside of her lip in self-reprimand for letting him think he was softening her up. He wasn't . . . not really. It was kind of sad about his mom, yeah. She would've freaked if her mother had left. But she wasn't going to give into those cute puppy dog eyes. No way.

"I bet you only believe me because I still find myself getting into trouble around you?"

She scowled; his smile fell.

Clearing his throat, he continued. "Anyway, my dad remarried my freshman year of college. I remember coming home for Christmas break and my room being . . . gone. He'd married a woman with two children." Meeting her gaze with a look she couldn't read, he added a side note. "The oldest starts college in a year. I took her senior picture yesterday." Glancing off again, he returned to his main story. "Mandy had already married Jeff and was pregnant with her firstborn at this point. But she set up a room for me, and I spent Christmas with her."

Sighing, he continued, "It's really weird. Sometimes, I'll run into my dad and my stepmom around town. We'll stop and talk a few minutes like a pair of old classmates who haven't seen each other since graduation. But it's nothing at all like I would've thought a relationship between father and son would be."

"No," she agreed. "It doesn't sound like it."

He lifted his gaze and something plopped

hard into her stomach. She wondered if it was her heart.

"Both my parents deserted me," he said. "Not that I really noticed it though. I always had Mandy. She's my only family. I'd do anything for her."

"I see," Mia murmured. And honestly, she did. It was sad because she realized how truly they stood on opposites sides of this issue between his brother-in-law and her roommate.

Though she understood just how much they could never be friends now, she held open the screen door for him. "Do you want to come in?"

His eyes lit with a yes, but he physically took a step back. "Is your roommate home?"

The distaste in his gaze had her back stiffening. She let the open gap in the door close a few inches. "Would it matter if she was?"

This wasn't going to work. Nothing between them could ever work. Disappointment sliced through her even as he ran his hand through his hair and murmured, "Why don't you come out here with me?"

"Honestly, Drew," she murmured. "What would that accomplish?"

His smile fell. He stared at her for five miserable seconds before saying, "I wonder if I could use the right words to describe how much I adore just looking at you. Every time I'm around you, it's like . . . everything goes on high alert. Concentrating on anything is impossible because I'm so —" He shivered and another smile sprouted on his lips.

Mia knew exactly what he meant. She felt the same thrill around him.

"Do you even feel a little of that in return?" he wondered, his gaze probing and intense.

Sucking in a breath, she made a momentous decision and stepped out onto the front steps with him. As the door shut behind her, his stunned expression made her smile.

"Thank you," he breathed out. "I like that answer."

She laughed, but the sound caught on a sob.

"No, no," he said quickly, reaching out. "Don't cry. I'm sorry."

He dropped his hand when she stiffened.

She whirled around, yanking open the door. "I'm sorry. This was a big mistake."

"Wait." He caught her elbow. "Mia." His thumb slid over sensitive skin on the inside of her arm, and she shivered. "I realize there's more going on here than I know about. And it's not just my suspicions about your roommate dating my brother-in-law." His fingers squeezed briefly before he whispered, "You have haunted eyes."

She pulled gently away and he let her go. Turning slowly, she lifted her haunted eyes to his baby blues. Compassion filled his gaze.

"I don't want to hurt you," he said. "But I can't ignore what's happening between us."

Opening her mouth to confess how her own feelings mirrored his, she stopped when he held up a hand. "Don't say anything yet. Wait until you've heard everything I have to say because . . . I did come over here today to coax information out of you about her."

Her jaw dropped. "You did?" That wasn't what she wanted to hear. She wanted more of his sweet confessions about how he liked being with her and looking at her.

"My sister's upset," he said, his eyes entreating. "She's completely distressed. I was ready to do anything I could for her. I still am. But as soon as you opened the door just now, I looked at you and realized I can't help her this way. I can't use you."

Not sure how to answer, she waited, letting him continue.

"So, I promise not to ask you any more questions about . . . about her if you just stay out here with me for a little while longer."

Temptation seized her. Caught in his blue gaze, she admitted, "She'll be home within the hour." Then he'd be forced to discover more information about Piper . . . or leave.

"Let's go out then. We'll just act like everyone else doesn't exist for a few hours. Let's pretend this is our first meeting."

She bit her lip. "I don't know."

His blue gaze seared into her. "Do you like pizza?"

After she gave a silent nod, he smiled and held out a hand. "It's almost supper time. If you come with me, we can be two people sharing a meal together and engaging in pleasant conversation."

Noticing how careful he tried not to make a big deal about it, she said, "But we won't call it a date, huh?"

"A date?" His brows lowered. "What's that?"

Rolling her eyes, she couldn't help but grin. But a split second later, indecision consumed her. He'd lied to her once and actually admitted he still wanted to spy on her roommate. Plus, there was that whole acceptance problem she needed to overcome but didn't want to try to overcome. She didn't know if she'd be able to make it through a date anyway. The whole idea screamed problems. But she was tempted. Oh, yeah, she was very tempted.

"I promise I'll keep my hands to myself," he added, raising his palms in surrender. "It's just eating. Everyone has to eat. Right?"

Mia licked her dry lips. "Okay, but we have to drive separately. And you can't follow me home afterward."

His eyes narrowed at the stipulations. But he gave a brief nod and said, "Deal."

"Could you please pass the parmesan?"

Realizing the bottle of grated cheese sat next to her elbow, Mia slid it across the restaurant table toward Drew.

"Thanks." He shot her a grin and shook out seasoning over the three slices of pizza sitting on his plate. And he continued to shake, covering the entire surface until barely any topping could be seen underneath.

She wrinkled her nose. "Would you like some more pizza to go with your cheese?"

He lifted his face, his expression completely innocent. "What?"

Swallowing her amusement, she said, "Nothing."

He motioned his finger toward the bottle

of red pepper seasoning next. "And that?" he asked.

Mia shook her head in disbelief. "No. You're not seriously going to mix parmesan cheese and red pepper together, are you?"

"What? It's good." He stretched forward, reaching past her to snag the pepper. Taking both shakers in hand, he hovered them above her single slice, threatening to tilt them. "Want to try it?"

"No!" She darted out her hand to stop him.

He chuckled and pulled the pepper and parmesan away. "Your loss." Then he proceeded to douse his supper again.

She wrinkled her nose. But a smile hovered over her lips, ready to turn into a full-blown laugh any second.

This was nice, she decided. Not at all nerve-wracking or frightening. She'd been afraid her first date after Ryan would be one of the most terrifying experiences of her life. In fact, she'd planned on never going through it . . . on being alone until she died. But Drew made dinner feel natural and relaxed. There was no panic at all. Contentment rippled through her. It was so surprising it felt foreign.

She could get used to being content, though, she thought. Yeah, contentment was definitely growing on her.

"Sure you don't want a taste test?" Drew asked, holding up both shakers and waggling them in a persuasive manner.

When she shook her head, he tsked in disapproval and set them on the table, nudging them her way to let her know they'd be right there in case she changed her mind.

And with that, he picked up a slice of pizza and half of it disappeared into his mouth. Watching him devour his food, she realized his parmesan/pepper offer wasn't merely about food, but everything about him. He showed her what she could have, made it look as appealing as he could, then set it aside, forcing no more pressure, all the while making it known she could still have it any time she changed her mind.

"Aren't you hungry?" he asked, pausing to eye her untouched food. His gaze lifted, concern thick in his voice.

Not wanting him to realize she'd been admiring him, she said, "I was just making sure that combination agreed with you. I was ready to perform CPR in case you keeled over."

He snorted. "This might surprise you, but it's perfectly normal to mix and match these two seasonings. I'm sure millions of other pizza-eaters in the world do the same thing. It tastes good."

"Hmm." Peeling off a section of pepperoni from her slice, she popped it into her mouth. "I'll just take your word for it," she answered as she chewed.

He watched her with glittering eyes as she chose another pepperoni. Pointing it out, he asked, "Do you always eat the topping first?"

At her nod, he shook his head. "See. That right there is strange to me. I don't have the patience to eat one pepperoni at a time."

She glanced at his half-consumed slice and chuckled. "I noticed."

"You're probably not a crust-eater either, are you?"

"Nope." After swallowing the last pepperoni on her piece, she finally took a nibble off the end.

"I call dibs on your crust then. I love dipping them in the marinara sauce."

Thinking about the intimacy of him eating her crust after she'd had her mouth all over it, she swallowed her next piece wrong and had to snag her drink from the table.

After polishing off his helping, Drew started piling more pizza on his plate. "So, tell me something about you," he said as he licked off a drop of sauce he'd smeared on his finger.

She straightened, alarmed by the question. He wanted to talk about her? She didn't want to talk about her. She didn't want him to know about her past. Not yet.

"What do you want to know?" she hedged, hoping her expression didn't show how worried she'd grown.

He shrugged. "I don't know. Everything. Start with what you do every day. You have a job, right?"

Her shoulders eased and she let out a quiet sigh of relief. Oh, thank God. An easy question. "Yes, I have a job."

Rolling his eyes, he added, "Of course," for her, since her tone implied as much. "So, what do you do?"

"I work for a telephone directory company. I handle selling the advertisements in the yellow pages."

"Interesting," he murmured. "I hadn't thought of placing an ad there yet. But I might now." Winking, he asked, "Think you could get me a discount on a full-page ad?"

"No way," she said. "I get commission."

He laughed. "Okay then." Setting his elbows on the table and resting his chin on his hands, he leaned forward. "So . . . have you always wanted to sell ads for a telephone directory?"

"Have you always wanted to be a photographer?" she countered, growing feisty.

He wrinkled his eyebrows as if that was an absurd question. "Well, yeah."

She laughed. "That's right. You want to see your pictures in *National Geographic*."

"You remember," he said softly.

Clearing her throat at the sudden familiarity that sprang up between them, she glanced away. "Why didn't you follow that dream?"

"Mandy," he answered so suddenly, she frowned and sent him a questioning look.

His smile looked forced. "She took it hard when I told her I wanted to travel. In fact, to keep me around, she offered me a loan to start a photography studio here in town. She'd also inherited the house I live in now when our grandma died. So, she deeded it over to me as an added incentive."

"But she didn't offer you a loan to do what you really wanted to do?" Mia asked. "To travel?"

Drew studied her silently. "No, she didn't," he murmured, sitting back to put space between them. "But I don't resent her for that. Not at all. She raised me. She did more for me than any sister should be expected to do. I owe her everything. And it's not like I hate my life. I like what I do. I like where I am. But —"

"You still wonder what it'd be like to photograph the four corners of the world," Mia finished for him.

His smile was slow but warm. "Exactly." Glancing down at his hand, he gave a soft laugh. "I always worried I was selfish for that. For wondering what if."

"I don't think you are."

He lifted his eyes. His booth shook, telling her he was nervously jiggling his knee under the table. There was a tormented glint in his gaze like he wanted to believe her but couldn't bring himself to forgive himself for his imperfection, though she didn't see it as such.

"Anyone need a refill?"

Mia jumped at the server's voice.

"I'm good," Drew answered and glanced across the table toward her. "How about you?"

"I'm fine," she answered, smiling up at the woman and wishing she'd leave already so she could talk more with Drew. He denied resenting his sister too vehemently. She wondered if he did hold something against Mandy. It made sense, since he felt so guilty about wondering what if.

But the mood had broken and his demeanor changed, telling her the subject was officially closed.

Grinning again, he said, "Enough about me. I want to know about you."

Walls went up immediately. Her gaze grew shuttered and she glanced down at her hands. "There's not much to tell."

"Well . . ." He wasn't going to let her off that easy. "Where're you from? That's a good place to explore next. Do you have any family?"

She grinned, relieved and delighted to get another easy question. "I'm from Chicago," she said. "I have both parents. They're still married and living there. No siblings."

He winced. "An only child, huh? You know what they say about them, don't you?"

She quirked a brow. "What? That we're all well-adjusted whiz kids?"

He chuckled. "That's not quite what I've heard."

Grinning, she retorted. "Then you've been listening to the wrong sources."

Obviously liking this flirtatious side of her, Drew moved closer. "I guess I have," he murmured and reached across the table to tuck a stray piece of honey blond hair behind her ear.

She sucked in a breath and her smile faltered. Her gaze skidded to his. His blue eyes showed disappointment at her with-drawal, but he casually dropped his hand

and slid back into relaxed mode.

"When did you move here?"

She blinked, gathering her scattered senses, and wondered if he was purposely trying to throw her off guard by abruptly changing subjects.

"About a year ago," she answered. "Piper invited me to come live with her. We'd been friends since second grade. She tried the college here, but dropped out and entered cosmetology school instead. Now, she styles hair."

He frowned. "You've been friends with her since grade school?" At her nod, the perplexity on his face deepened. "Really? Hmm. You guys don't seem like the same type at all." Not wanting to talk about her roommate with him, her eyes coated and the blockade went up. He seemed to realize he'd brought up a prohibited topic, though, because he dropped it just as suddenly and sent her an ornery look.

"Okay, one last question." Ignoring her leery frown, he asked, "Have you ever dated anyone as amazing as me?"

For a moment, she merely gaped, thinking he was serious. Then she threw her head back and laughed. "Why, of course not," she gave him the answer she knew he wanted. "I've never even met anyone as amazing as you."

He sat back in the booth, looking smug. "That's what I thought."

CHAPTER NINE

As Drew walked Mia to her car, he made sure to stay close enough for their arms to brush every few steps. He figured it was progress when she didn't step away. The woman was a puzzle. At times, he didn't think she wanted to be happy. Then he'd manage to coax a smile out of her and things went great for a few minutes, until something happened as if reminding her she needed to return to miserable. And she'd withdraw, starting the cycle over again.

He tried not to push, but the curiosity was killing him. He wanted to know why? Why did she shy away from pleasure? Why did she feel so convinced she had to be depressed? He guarded his words, measuring everything before he spoke, hoping he didn't trigger another decline because, well, he liked it when she slipped up and smiled for him.

"So," he said, keeping his hands in his

pockets so they wouldn't stray and do something to upset her. "Think you'll get hungry again in the next week or so?"

Eyes glittering, she asked, "Are you trying to ask me out on another non-date?"

He feigned appalled shock. "Of course not. That was the furthest thing from my mind. How could you even suggest such an idea?"

Amusement tickled the corner of her mouth. She paused at her Nissan, unlocking it before turning to face him. "Can I ask you something?"

He inched closer until she had to tip her head up to meet his gaze. God, he liked looking down on her. "You can ask me anything."

Looking uncertain at first, she daintily cleared her throat. "Why are you even bothering? You know this can't go anywhere."

Pulling back, he blinked in surprise. "Actually, I don't know that. Why can't it go anywhere?"

Letting out a small sigh, she said, "Think about it, Drew. You've lied to me from the very first moment we met."

His mouth fell open. "I have not. Since the moment I confessed everything at the studio, I haven't lied once. And you know why I had to lie when we first met. My sister was counting on me. She's still counting on me, in fact. She so rarely asks anything of me. When she begged me to find out what her husband was up to, there was no way I could say no."

"She . . . she asked you to do that?"

He shifted uneasily. How had the tables turned to make him the bad guy? She was the one with the cheating roommate. She was the one protecting her precious Piper. He was just trying to be a good brother.

"Yes," he said, unable to entirely erase the defensive note from his voice. "She asked me to help her. And I did. I still will."

Mia shook her head, looking confused. "Why can't she just approach her husband about it?"

Drew gave a half-hearted shrug. "I'm not exactly sure. I keep asking her the same question, and she always has a different answer. I think she's scared. She doesn't want him to know she's suspicious in case she ends up being wrong. But . . . I don't think she wants to hear the truth from him even if she was certain. That would make it too real for her."

Mia nodded. "Okay, I can understand that. If I heard bad news from someone who wasn't directly involved, then I could still doubt its legitimacy because it didn't come straight from the source. It's a defense mechanism. She's guarding herself, and I can't fault her for that either. I'd probably do the same thing."

She would, would she? Drew tipped his head and eyed her curiously. "You wouldn't ask your husband about it if you thought he was two-timing?"

"No," she answered. "I don't believe I would, now that I've thought it through."

"Hmm," he murmured. "That's strange. I'd confront my wife. I don't think I could marry someone unless I could talk about anything with her."

"Even if it's something you knew would hurt her?" she asked. At his sharp look, she lifted her hands in surrender. "Sorry. I was just playing devil's advocate."

"No," he told her. "You're fine. That was actually a good question because I don't know what I'd do now that you put it that way."

No way could he hurt the woman he loved by telling her she looked fat in a certain outfit, so why would he needlessly hurt her with adultery questions . . . except, thinking your spouse was cheating was a far cry from telling her she looked chubby.

"I don't know what I'd do," he said, shak-

157

ing his head. "All I know is that Mandy asked me to help her. And that's what I'm going to do."

"So, you still plan on using me to get information."

He frowned. "Of course not. I already told you I wouldn't. I just . . . I'll find some other way."

"Are you going to ask your brother-in-law about it then?"

He paused. "I don't know." Probably not. If Mandy refused to confront him, then she had a reason for it and he'd negate her reasons if he talked to Jeff.

"But I swear I won't go through you."

She pulled her bottom lip through her teeth and swayed forward. "I like that answer."

He shifted toward her. "Do you? How much?"

Lashes fluttered closed, she murmured, "This much," and leaned into him with her mouth pursed. From that point on, he was lost.

When his lips touched hers, she whimpered and reached out to wrap her hand around the back of his neck. The ends of his hair curled over her fingers, silky soft and warm.

She sighed, unsure. He tasted like pizza,

parmesan cheese and red pepper. And, yum, the flavor wasn't so bad after all.

Gently, he touched the side of her neck. His fingers barely skimmed over her erratic pulse. Then they drifted down to the very top of her chest, where they followed her shoulder blade to the top of her arm. Pausing his caress at her elbow, he stepped closer.

"You're so soft," he murmured against her mouth, pulling away long enough to watch his hand slide from her elbow to her wrist and then tangle his fingers through hers. It caused a shiver to race up the back of her neck.

His eyes shot to hers; the heat in their blue depths made her breathless and light-headed. He dipped his head again. She kept her eyes open long enough to watch his face grow closer and his lashes sweep over his cheeks. Then he kissed her.

Closing the last three inches separating them, Mia leaned against him. She felt it all the way to the tips of her toes; it exploded out every nerve ending on the way down.

This was the first thrill she'd experienced in three years. And even then, it was stronger than any kiss she'd had before. The jolt terrified her.

She broke away. Covering her trembling

lips, she stared at him with a wide gaze. His gaze was heavy-lidded. His chest moved in and out, and he blinked a few times before he seemed to return to his senses.

Then he reached out, touched her elbow lightly and asked, "Are you okay?"

She nodded, keeping her hands firmly over her mouth. He dropped his hand.

"You look scared."

She was scared. "I'm fine," she said, the words were muffled behind her palm. Lowering her hands to her chin, she repeated, "I'm fine. I'm sorry I —"

"Don't apologize. It's okay. I shouldn't have rushed you."

"You didn't —"

Reaching to touch her check, he cut her off mid-word. "Can I call you sometime?"

Mia blinked, totally confounded by this man. Here, he'd practically been eating her alive and she'd loved every minute of it. Then he backpedaled. How did he know she needed to go so slow?

She nodded, unable to deny him anything.

He grinned. "Good." Then he leaned forward and pecked a quick kiss to her forehead. "And you're wrong," he murmured in her ear. "This can go somewhere."

Walking on air, Drew unlocked his back

door and entered the dark kitchen, flipping a light on as he went. He couldn't seem to stop grinning. Floating to his fridge, he pulled it open and dug out a bottle of water. Twisting off the cap, he chugged the entire thing, gulping until it was empty.

Beaming as he threw his bottle in the plastic recycling can Amanda had set up for him, he wiped his mouth with his hand and swore he could still taste Mia.

This could go somewhere. Oh, yes, it could. And it would.

He'd barely plopped down in a kitchen chair when his business line rang in the other sitting room. Immediately, he wondered if it was Mia. She'd found his house from the business card he'd given her. That was no doubt the only number of his she had. And he'd asked if he could call her. Maybe she was taking the initiative and calling him.

As he hurried into the other room, he told himself not to expect her. It was just a customer calling. It wasn't Mia.

But as he answered, he tensed in expectation.

"Harper Studio."

"Where have you been?" his sister snapped, sounding annoyed.

His shoulders slumped in disappointment.

"Your cell phone's turned off; I've been trying to reach you for the past two hours."

"I was out," he answered evasively, well aware she'd freak if he told her he'd been with Mia and not gleaning any information about her roommate.

"Well, I finally talked to him."

He froze. She'd talked to Jeff? Already?

It was too soon. Though he'd been wishing she'd hurry and confront him already, after the evening he'd spent with Mia, he wasn't so anxious anymore. He had a bad feeling there'd be a line drawn and he and Mia would end up on opposite sides. He wasn't ready yet.

"About time," he said. "What'd he say?"

"He got really upset about the whole idea that his own wife didn't trust him. We had a huge fight. And he told me his boss had asked him to take a business trip to Denver next weekend. He'd declined before, but now he thinks he wants to go . . . I think he meant it to punish me because I asked him if he was having an affair. But he's going to be gone for the girls' end of the year music program, Drew. They've been excited about this for weeks. And he won't be there."

Drew had forgotten all about that program. He'd already promised Natalie and Lucy he'd go to it. Bluck.

"What'd he say about the flower delivery?"

His sister paused before answering and he had a sinking feeling he wasn't going to like her answer.

"He said the flower shop must've delivered them to the wrong address."

Closing his eyes, he cursed under his breath. "Mandy, that's not a very good excuse."

"Gee, you think?"

"Who'd he say he was trying to send them to?"

She groaned. "He said they were for his mom. I don't believe that though. Why would a man send his mother red roses?"

Drew didn't buy the excuse either. He ran his fingers through his hair, hating this. Jeff was cheating on Amanda. It was starting to feel more and more real. Fingers tingling, he switched hands on the phone and flexed his arm, wishing he could do something to stop the hopelessness surging through him.

"Have you found anything out from the roommate?" Amanda asked.

Drew ground his teeth. "I . . . No, not yet."

He couldn't tell her there was no way he'd use Mia like that. She wouldn't betray her best friend for some guy she hardly knew,

163

anyway. It had been wrong to ask that of her.

"But I'll find out something on my end," he said. "I promise."

There had to be some other way to investigate.

He'd better get the brother of the year award for this, Drew thought bitterly as he pushed into Styles R Us Hair Salon a week later. Two women glanced up from the magazines they were thumbing through as they sat with crossed legs in the waiting area. Behind them, in the tiled section, one hairdresser had her customer's head tipped back over a sink as she rinsed soapy red locks and another hairdresser clipped away a little girl's bangs. He didn't see Mia's roommate anywhere.

The female-dominated place didn't ease his nerves, and he wondered how Jeff could stand getting his hair cut here.

Since he didn't spot Piper right away, he decided not to stick around and was already reaching for the door handle when he heard her voice.

"Drew?"

Reluctantly, he paused and turned. Coming through a doorway covered with a pink curtain, Piper grinned and approached. "I thought that was you. How are you?"

His gut burned as he studied her. He could almost picture her wrapped around Jeff.

"What a surprise," she said. "Have you come to get a haircut?"

There was no telling what Mia had already told her roommate about him. By the way she smiled, though, he had to think not too much. She probably didn't know he was Jeff's brother-in-law . . . It was either that or she didn't even know who Jeff was, though he had a bad feeling she did.

"Uh . . ." Not sure which question to answer first, he settled for what he hoped looked like a friendly smile.

"If you need a trim," she said, "I've got an opening. Come on back."

He paused, not wanting a haircut. He liked to keep his locks long enough to curl. When he was little, his mother hated his curls, saying they made him look like a girl. She'd kept his head practically shaved. After she walked out, he made a point to grow the curls as long as he could stand. It was probably a stupid rebellion since his mother didn't even know he did it, but he couldn't seem to stop.

"No thanks," he told Mia's roommate. "I, uh . . . Actually, I, came in here to talk to you about Mia."

She cocked her head and sent him a questioning look. "You already knew I worked here?"

He opened his mouth and floundered a second. Then he gave a shrug. "She mentioned it."

When she smiled, his tense muscles loosened. He hoped she'd think he meant Mia when he said "she." No way was he telling her Amanda had mentioned it first.

"Well, I'd love to talk to you about Mia," she said before pausing. "Sure you don't want a trim while we're at it? Like I said, it's pretty dead around this place right now. And I'll do it for a discount since you're Mia's friend."

His hand went protectively to his hair. "I'm okay."

She just smiled as she studied his mane. "I have a really good idea of something to do with it," she coaxed.

His eyes widened as he pictured Mohawks and dreadlocks.

She chuckled, reading his expression. "Come on back." She waved him to follow. "I promise you'll like it. I'm not going to shave you bald."

He swallowed. "How much are you going to take off?"

166

"I'm just going to reshape. I think you should look less like David Hasselhoff and more like Tate Donovan."

She rolled her eyes. Lifting her hand like she was taking an oath on a bible, she swore, "It'll look great. I promise."

He started to follow until he realized what he was doing. Mandy would slaughter him if she knew he was letting Jeff's supposed mistress anywhere near his hair. She used to comb it back when he'd been too young to care about doing that himself. Letting Piper touch it felt like he was cheating on his sister too.

"Drew-eww?" she sung his name in a coaxing taunt. "Do you want to talk about Mia or not?"

He clenched his teeth. "Oh, all right." This was for Mandy, he told himself as he slowly came forward. Mandy. And okay, he wanted to get some advice on Mia too. He'd love to know what had happened to make her so skittish.

Piper beamed, triumphant. "Now we're talking."

CHAPTER TEN

"So, Mia huh?"

Drew cracked open one eye. A droplet of rinse water dribbled down the back of his neck and inside the plastic cape Piper had bibbed around him. When a second followed, he squirmed.

"First things first," Piper said, she pressed down on the silver lever by his feet and his seat sank. "How serious about her are you?"

He blinked. "Well . . . I've only met her a few times." But they'd been very significant encounters, each leaving him a little more lost in his fixation.

"But you're interested enough to come talk to me about her," Piper urged as she snipped off his first chuck of hair in the back.

Frowning as he tried to watch her in the mirror, he answered, "Right."

He tensed when she clipped away another chunk, thinking this was a very bad idea.

He didn't want to lose his curls. They'd grown on him in the past twenty-some years.

"What exactly were you planning on learning from me?" Piper asked, going to town now back there.

Since he couldn't ask if she was dating his brother-in-law while she had scissors in her hand, he said, "Do you know why she's —" Caught on what would be the best word to use, he paused, unable to think one up.

"Why she's what?" Piper demanded, sounding extremely defensive.

He sighed. "I don't know how to explain it. She's perfect in every way. But it's like . . . like . . ." Might as well say it straight, he decided as he finished, "It's like she doesn't want to be happy sometimes. We'll get to talking and she'll be smiling and even laughing. Then, bam. She realizes she's having too much fun and purposely tones it down."

He hated it. She really was perfect in every way. Beautiful, sweet, intuitive. And they connected. There were definite sparks. But she was purposely holding herself back. He just wanted to grab her shoulders and shake that stubbornness out of her. They could have something so amazing if she'd just allow it to happen.

"You're right," Piper answered morosely. "She doesn't want to smile. Being happy hurts her."

Drew twisted his head up to see Piper's face, but she caught his skull, moved his head back to where she wanted him, and cut off another chunk. He stayed immobile.

"Why doesn't she want to be happy?" he asked, growing impatient with this whole hair-cutting nonsense.

"Something happened to her."

"What?" he butted in.

"Something happened to her," she repeated a bit louder this time. "About three years ago and it still affects her. She suffers from survivor's guilt."

He sucked in a breath. "Survivor's guilt? You mean someone close to her died?" When she didn't answer soon enough, he impatiently asked, "Who?"

"Someone extremely close to her," Piper said.

His mind spun. A boyfriend. It was the only explanation he could come up with. She'd been in love with some other guy, and now he was dead. She probably still mourned him. Jealously roared through Drew, and he couldn't help but wonder if she'd thought about the other guy when she'd kissed him.

He shuddered, hating that idea. But it certainly explained why she froze up when he got too close. It was no wonder she needed to go slow. He did speculate though, how her boyfriend had died. It must've been traumatic, maybe even partly her fault. Maybe she'd been driving the car when he'd been killed in an automobile accident.

Ideas raced through him and he stared blindly ahead, wishing Piper would just tell him the rest of it, yet fearing it too. He didn't particularly want to hear about some other guy if Mia had been so into him.

No way was he going to ask though. He had this unreasonable fear she'd cut his throat with one of those old-time shaving knives if he pressed too much or said the wrong thing.

Yeah, okay, he'd seen too many mobster movies.

"I'm done," she said, unsnapping the cape from around his neck and carefully pulling it off him so it'd catch most of his cut hair.

Spinning his chair around, she had him face the wall of mirrors. "What do you think?"

He gaped at his reflection, amazed. She'd been right. It wasn't exactly short, though it wasn't as long as it had been. It looked totally different. Restructured. Unable to help himself, he reached up to touch it, making sure it was really his hair.

"Not too bad," he murmured.

"Yeah, I'm pretty handy with scissors," she said. "Don't hurt my roommate and I won't show you what else I can do with them."

Freezing, he met her eyes in the mirror. Then he lifted his face. "Excuse me?"

There was no way he'd heard that right.

Her brown gaze was dead serious. "Mia's my best friend in the entire world. And she's been through a living nightmare. If you don't go slow enough or if you push her into something she's not ready for, you'll regret it. I'll make sure you regret it."

Swallowing, he gave a brief nod. "Message received." It was nice Mia had such a faithful friend. But anger spiked through him at her self-righteous attitude, like she was the upstanding, good guy here.

He wasn't the one involved with a married man. He wasn't the one hurting a mother of three and making her paranoid and bitter. He wasn't the one breaking apart a family.

Suddenly remembering he was here for Mandy, not Mia, he studied Piper's face, trying to think up something to say to dig into her head and find out her deepest secrets.

"I won't hurt her," he murmured.

"Good." Smiling regally, Piper patted his shoulder. "Now that that's taken care of, you owe me twenty bucks."

For a second he could only gawk at her. Twenty bucks? That was a discount? He usually got it done for twelve at the barber shop across town.

But he didn't argue. He wanted to get away from this woman, because every second in her presence only made him feel nastier.

He dug into his wallet and found two tens. As he silently handed them over, he noticed the rock sparkling from the index finger on her right hand. Caught, staring at it, he swallowed.

"Nice ring." He glanced up, remembering how good Jeff was at giving jewelry. Mandy usually received some kind of trinket every birthday and anniversary.

Piper lifted her fingers to touch the ring in a loving caress, and he gained enough confidence to ask, "From someone special?"

Proudly, she answered, "Yes."

Nauseated, he was unable to stop himself as he asked, "From J?"

Her eyes opened wide, and her face

drained of color. "Mia told you about him?"

His insides went still. He was so close now. If only he played his cards right; he might get what he wanted. "I saw your roses."

Her shoulders relaxed. "Worried they were for Mia, were you?"

"Something like that," he confessed. More worried who they'd been from actually.

"Yeah, my Sugar Daddy sent those a few weeks ago. Just because."

Drew's eyebrows rose as if he were interested, though, he really just felt ill. "A sugar daddy, huh? So, he's older?"

Flaunting a feminine smile that hid centuries of secrets, she admitted, "A little."

Is he married, he ached to ask. Are you seeing a married man? Are you seeing my sister's husband?

He couldn't do it though. He was right there, on the brink, and he choked.

Mia's face flickered through his head and he could see her confused, hurt eyes as she realized he'd cornered her friend and grilled her.

Gritting his teeth, he nodded to Piper. "Have a good day." He saw her perplexed expression, no doubt wondering why he decided to leave in the middle of a conversation. But he couldn't talk to her anymore. Couldn't even look at her. Spinning away, he hurried for the exit.

It wasn't until he reached his truck and slid into the driver's seat that he realized . . . Mia might be pleased with his decision. But Amanda certainly wouldn't be.

He closed his eyes and hissed a curse, wishing there was an easy answer.

Drew waited three days to call Mia. Though he'd gone for the whole proper, patient thing, patience really didn't work so well for him. He'd almost called about a dozen different times, half of those occasions on the night they'd gone to the pizza parlor. The need had only grown worse after talking to her roommate. He didn't much care for Piper Holliday. He might like the new look she gave him, but he felt more certain than ever that she was involved with Jeff.

Deciding not to tell Amanda about his haircut experience since he hadn't learned anything concrete, he stayed away from the Wright house, half afraid his sister would ask another impossible favor of him. He wasn't equipped for this PI stuff. In fact, he was tempted to look one up and hire the guy to find out what was going on.

Mia's number was in the phone book under her roommate's name. He still wasn't sure about her last name. Maybe he'd find out pretty soon.

It rang three times and Piper answered. "Hello?"

He winced. So not the person he wanted to hear. "Is Mia there?"

"She sure is, Drew," the roommate told him, making his wince deepen because she recognized his voice. "Hold on a sec."

She didn't cover the mouthpiece as she yelled, "Mi Mi. It's Drew."

Very clearly, he heard Mia answer, "I'll take it in the other room."

He grinned. Yes! She wanted to talk to him in private. Always a plus.

Then she answered. "Hello."

"Hey," he said. "I was just calling to see if you might possibly be hungry."

It took her a second to answer. When he heard the click on the line, signifying Piper had hung up on her end, Mia finally said, "You talked to Piper."

He paused. "Well, yeah. She answered the phone."

"No. Not that. She told me she cut your hair a few days ago."

He winced. Yikes. She did not sound happy. She must've only wanted to berate him in private.

"You asked her about her flowers."

"Oh," he said. "That. Yeah, I did."

176

"I thought you said you weren't going to pry information out of us."

He closed his eyes. "I said I wouldn't pry information out of you, Mia. Your roommate's a completely different matter."

"Well, I don't think she is."

He groaned, clenching his teeth. Did they really have to talk about this right now? He'd like a few days where he didn't have to think about adultery or uncovering secrets.

"Don't ever talk to her again," Mia said, her voice cold and authoritative.

"So, if I run into her on the street someday, I'm just supposcd to turn my back and be rude?"

"You know what I mean," she growled. "Don't try any more of your underhanded —"

"How can you protect her?" he exploded, thinking this was ridiculous. "She's breaking up a marriage. She's —"

"You don't know that."

"But you do," he shot back. "And yet you're still defending her."

"Piper is my friend," she muttered.

"Yeah, well, I have lots of friends that do things I don't approve of, and I call them on it. To me, that's a real friend."

"Oh, so now you're questioning my eth-

177

ics?" She sounded so insulted, he winced.

"No," he backtracked. "That's not what I'm doing. I'm . . . dang it. I don't know what I'm doing. I just know I've been stuck in the middle of something I shouldn't even be involved in."

"So am I," Mia shot back.

"You are," he agreed. "We're both innocent, unwilling participants. So, why are we arguing?"

Her voice sounded calmer as she answered, "Because we've been shoved on opposite sides of the conflict."

"Yeah," he murmured, confused. "And why is that?"

"Because my friend, who I'm loyal to, is on one side and your sister, who you're extremely loyal to, is on the other."

He nodded in understanding. "But what if I feel like I'm growing extremely loyal to you?"

She sounded sad as she admitted, "That's why this is so hard."

He pressed his forehead against the wall, pleased she'd experienced the growing-close thing too, yet utterly frustrated because there was still nothing to do about it.

"I can't stop thinking about you," he admitted. "I don't care about the obstacles. I want to see you again."

She gave a groan. "I don't think that's a good idea."

Gnashing his teeth, he said, "Why? Because you think I'm spying on your roommate?"

"Are you?"

He swallowed. "Mia, I'm not using you. I swear. I just want to get to know you."

"And you totally just avoided my question."

"There's something between us," he pushed. "Every time we're together . . ."

"Don't go there, Drew."

"You already told me you feel it too."

"I'm hanging up now. Don't call again."

"Mia —"

She hung up, and he cursed, tossing the phone onto his bed.

CHAPTER ELEVEN

Though it wasn't her turn to buy groceries, Mia needed an excuse to get away. Every time the phone rang, she jumped, hoping it wasn't Drew, yet hoping it was.

She pushed her cart around a corner of the cereal aisle and almost ran smack into an oncoming shopper.

"Sorry," she gasped and stumbled to a stop just in time.

"No problem," a male voice answered. "I should start watching where I'm going one of these days."

She looked up and then up some more. With sandy, blond hair and a healthy tan, the man in front of her pulled his cart back a few inches, giving her room to move past. He was tall, a good six inches taller than Drew.

Gritting her teeth, Mia told herself not to compare. Stop thinking about Drew. But she couldn't help but notice differences.

A pair of curious brown eyes inspected her. "Go ahead," he offered.

She murmured a thank you and dropped her eyes as she skirted around him. He turned to openly inspect her as she went. Not sure what to make of this, she rushed by and hurried down the next aisle, escaping his perusal.

Four years ago, getting checked out wouldn't have made her so uncomfortable. But these days she was intensely aware of every time male eyes shifted her way. Directly after the funeral, she'd been too steeped in misery to even notice the outside world. But lately, she spotted everything and everyone. Such awareness told her she was finally at that stage, the stage where she was beginning to move on.

Pausing, Mia lifted her face. She was beginning to accept.

No, she thought, becoming panicked. No, she wasn't ready. She couldn't accept. She couldn't let go. What kind of awful person would that make her if she moved on?

Clutching her cart in a death grip, she glanced at the rows of neatly stocked baby food surrounding her. Tears prickled her eyes. Oh, God, she really was moving on.

She needed to get out of here. Whipping her cart around, she nearly rammed into a floor display of Huggies. A sob caught in her throat. A year ago, the sight of diapers would've made her hyperventilate.

It was so upsetting, she wanted to scream. But the center of the grocery story was so not the place for a panic attack. Thinking to buy what she'd collected so far and get home, she started for the checkout lane and really did bump into another shopper.

"Sorry," she said breathlessly and glanced up long enough to notice it was the same guy she'd collided with before. "Again," she added on a belated note and tried to steer around him.

Instead of appearing irritated by her, he grinned. "We really gotta stop meeting like this."

She offered him a vague smile. When she realized she couldn't squeeze past him, she stepped aside to let him go first. If he didn't move soon, she was going to have a full-blown breakdown right here in the baby aisle of the IGA.

The man moved out of her way. "Go ahead," he offered. "Ladies first."

"Thanks," she said, hurrying forward.

"My name's Gary, by the way. Gary Davis."

"Oh." She jerked around, surprised he'd followed her and even more surprised he thought they were still talking. "Hi," she offered. "I'm Mia." And I really need to get out of here.

He held out a long, tanned arm. "Nice to meet you."

Great. Not only did the guy have to remind her she was healing by checking her out, but he had to go and flirt with her too.

Tall and wide, he was a nice-looking gentlemen, with a wide forehead that made him look extra male and dark, brown eyes set deep in his eyes to give him a shadowed look. So very unlike Drew. He'd be just the type to help her get over Drew . . . if she hadn't already decided she was never going on another date for the rest of her life.

Grinning, Gary picked up her hand before she could decide whether she wanted to shake with him or not. He slowly pumped their palms up and down. "Come here often?" he asked. Amusement twinkled in his eyes as if he'd just told a joke.

She didn't catch it. "Ah . . . Every time I need groceries," she answered.

Laughing, he finally let go of her. "Would it be tacky if I asked you to go out for a drink sometime?"

Mia froze.

"Are you ready to try the next step?" she could hear Dr. Higgins' voice echo though her. As much as she didn't want to be ready to move on, she knew she'd already started making that step.

It had begun.

Gary waited patiently. "What do you say?" he coaxed softly.

It wasn't like this would be her first date since the tragedy anyway. She'd eaten pizza with Drew. He'd insisted on paying and they'd kissed afterward. That was a fairly date-worthy description. She'd taken the first step toward acceptance. Every other date now should be a hundred times easier. There was no way she would go out with Drew Harper again either, so . . .

She needed to do this. If she was going to make it through the rest of her life, she needed to move on, no matter how much it hurt.

"Sure," she said and sent him a wavering smile. "I'd like that."

His eyes lit with surprise. "Really? I mean, yeah. Okay. That's cool. When's a good time for you?"

She shrugged. "Oh . . . any time." Probably as soon as they could manage would be best so she didn't have time to chicken out. "What do you prefer?"

He sent her a shrug. "This Friday? Club 808?"

Nodding, she repeated, "Friday it is."

"Great. Where do you live? I'll pick you up."

"Where do I —" Growing abruptly anxious, she shook her head. "How about I just meet you there. Six sound okay?"

Okay, maybe she wasn't as ready as she thought she was.

Mia examined herself in the hall mirror and bit her lip. Her stomach wouldn't stop churning; it made her nauseous. This didn't feel right. Nerves hadn't plagued her during her dinner with Drew. Then again, she hadn't planned nearly a week ahead of time with him. She hadn't needed to dress up or build suspense. It had just happened, and it had been fun and casual and the most perfect evening she'd spent with anyone in a long time.

And if she didn't quit thinking about it, she was going to be in big trouble. Drew was the past. Plus he was all wrong for her. Though she had to admit, his determination to help his sister was admirable; that was the exact reason she couldn't see him anymore.

"Wow, you look nice. Are you seeing Drew again?"

Dreamy smile falling flat, she turned from

the mirror. Piper stood paused in the door-way to her room, looking stunned as she scanned Mia's dress. Her mouth was an O and her eyebrows raised.

"No," she answered. "I'm not seeing Drew. I'm meeting someone else at 808's for a drink."

"Holy cow." Piper's O turned from a lowercase to a capital. Hurrying forward, she took Mia's hand and clutched it eagerly. "What happened to Drew? Who's this new guy? I can't believe this! It's like my old Mi Mi's returning."

Mia paused. Was she really turning into the old Mi Mi? Did she even want to be that woman again? Things had changed too much. She wanted to stop hurting, but she didn't really care to go back to who she was before. She just wanted to be someone new.

"I've been out a lot these past few days, I know, but I can't believe I missed this much," Piper ranted. "Now, spill it. Who's the new guy? And what happened to Drew? I liked Drew."

Biting the inside of her lip, Mia wondered if Piper would like Drew so much if she knew he was J's wife's brother.

"Where have you been?" Mia asked changing the subject. Anything to divert the focus off her.

Piper wavered, looking suddenly reluctant. Glancing away, she motioned blindly. "Oh, here and there. Dating someone new."

Mia froze. "Really? That's wonderful," she said with so much enthusiasm her roommate blinked in confusion. "I mean, I'm glad you've moved past . . . the married guy."

"Yeah," Piper admitted, sighing as she glanced away. "But enough about me. Who's your new guy?"

"Oh." Right, new guy. Shoot, she'd forgotten his name. "Gary!" she exclaimed a moment later, snapping her fingers in relief. *Gary. Don't forget Gary.* "Gary Davis."

Piper's smile dropped flat. "Gary Davis?" she repeated. "I know Gary."

Mia frowned. "You do? How?"

"We dated the first year I moved here," Piper answered, shaking her head over the coincidence. "Shared a history class in college. He was working toward his bachelor's in Electrical Engineering. Wow. That's so funny you met him. What a small world."

Mia's shoulders slumped. "He's one of your exes?"

Piper rolled her eyes. "That was a long time ago, Mi Mi. I haven't even talked to him in years. He was just a college football player back then. Kind of immature." Her

187

eyes widened as soon as she admitted that. Reaching for Mia's arm, she quickly reassured. "But that was a long time ago. I'm sure he's grown up a lot since then."

Still. Mia wasn't into sharing with her roommate "How . . . how serious did you guys get?"

"Well," Piper looked momentarily uneasy. "It was a long time ago," she finally admitted.

Mia winced. "But you and he . . . were together?"

"Mia." Piper drew out a breath, sounding almost embarrassed, though she'd never been embarrassed before. "It was a long time ago."

"I don't care," Mia said. "That's just . . ."

Piper groaned and threw her hands in the air. "Great. You're not going to go out with him now, are you?"

Mia wrinkled her nose. "Well, honestly, how can I? It's so weird."

Her roommate sighed, shoulders slumping in defeat. "I knew it," she muttered. "I knew you'd come up with some reason not to go out. Yes, I dated Gary eons ago. So, what? He's still a good guy. And what about Drew? What was the problem there? Why don't you want to see him again?"

Glancing away, Mia gave a shrug. No way

was she going to confess how Drew wanted to use her to discover Piper's secrets. "You want to know what I think?" Piper went on when she didn't answer. "I think you're scared of him because he was the first guy to make you feel alive again after —"

"I don't want to talk about it," Mia snapped before Piper could finish her sentence. She closed her eyes and lifted her hands. "I just can't."

"Are you even going to call Gary and tell him you can't meet him?"

"I don't know his number," Mia confessed.

Piper snorted. "This is driving me crazy, Mia. Sometimes I can't handle watching you do this. You'll get so close to improving, and I'll feel so proud. Then a snap of the fingers later, you regress. I can't take it anymore. I just wish you'd —" She broke off and sent Mia a guilty look. After a long sigh, she finished, "I'm sorry. I don't mean to upset you. I just —"

"I understand," Mia murmured. She reached out and touched Piper's arm. Her roommate appeared stunned by the move. She glanced at Mia's hand, and her shoulders eased.

"It frustrates me too," Mia said.

"No, don't get frustrated. Don't listen to

189

me," Piper said, placing her hand over Mia's and pressing. "I should be commending you, not complaining. You've done so good lately. I'm really impressed."

"Yeah," Mia agreed softly. "I'm amazed too."

It had started because of Drew, though. Drew, who'd made her want to live again and then turned out to be an enemy.

As if growing uncomfortable with the deepening mood growing between them, Piper cleared her throat and stepped back. "Well, I'm headed off for the evening. I'll see you later . . . maybe tomorrow."

Mia nodded. "Have fun."

"Oh, I will," Piper assured. Then she waved and started for the exit. "Tootles."

Shaking her head, Mia decided her friend was acting perfectly typical. They could be in the middle of a conversation and she'd change tracks in a heartbeat, shifting gears and leaving or changing the subject.

Mia grinned for a second. At least something was still normal. But as she thought about being normal again, Drew's face wavered into her head. Smile dropping, she started for the phone and dialed a number she'd memorized from a certain business card.

"Harper Studio," that oh-so-familiar voice

answered.

Her heart skipped a beat. Oh, great. He still affected her like no one else ever had. Gritting her teeth, she growled, "I just want you to know you're wrong."

There was a pause and then, "Excuse me?" He sounded totally baffled.

"My roommate isn't dating your brother-in-law. Okay?" At least he wasn't dating her anymore, which was all that mattered to Mia.

She heard his breath catch. "Mia. What — you mean, you didn't know the truth yourself until just now?"

She growled. He wasn't supposed to assume that. He was supposed to be apologetic for causing such a stir . . . for believing the worst about her best friend . . . for upsetting her and trying to use her. He wasn't supposed to be happy.

"Ohhh, never mind," she muttered, too frustrated to berate him.

Hanging up before he could give any kind of excuse, Mia jumped when the phone rang only seconds after disconnecting. When she saw the Harper Studio number blink across her caller ID, she ignored it. Five rings later, the answering machine picked up and after Piper told him to leave a message . . . he did.

"Mia, will you please pick up and talk to me?"

She gasped. He was actually going to leave a message? She picked up the phone and disconnected. While she erased his message, he called again. She turned off the ringer and then the answering machine.

She backed up, staring at the phone as if daring it to ring now. When it didn't, she wondered if he'd try coming over.

Not wanting to stick around for that, she snagged her keys and purse off an end table and booked it out of there. Once she was in her car, she wasn't sure where to go, so she decided to meet Gary anyway and let him know her change in plans. Not that there'd been a big change. She'd always carried reservations about going out with him. Moving on didn't seem so easy or desirable when it was Gary she was supposed to meet.

That had to be the most depressing factor in her decision to dislike Drew. Even after he'd lied to her and then admitted he still wanted to expose her roommate, he continued to affect her more than all the others. Why that was remained a mystery.

Once she reached Club 808, she found a spot to park and gathered her purse close as she walked to meet Gary inside. She was still decked out in her nice clothes. A knee-length black skirt and flowery short-sleeved shirt. Conservative yet cute.

Once she reached the gated exterior where she could peek in and see the outside seating, she paused when she caught sight of Gary . . . with Piper.

Piper?

What the —

"Thanks for explaining everything to me, Piper," Gary clutched her upper arm and sent her a warm smile.

They stood close, like they knew each other well. Too well. His head tilted down intimately beside Piper's and she looked up at him, appearing very concerned as she bit her lip and asked, "So, you're not mad at her for standing you up?"

He shook his head. "No, of course not. After you just told me what happened to her, I understand her reservations. No hard feelings." He held up his hands as if that proved it. "I swear."

Obviously relieved, Piper's chest heaved as she puffed out a breath. Then she threw herself at him and hugged him hard, closing her eyes as she rested her face on his chest. "Thank you. Thank you so much, Gary. You have no idea what this means to me. She's a great person, she really is. She's just going through a hard time right now."

Lifting her head, she glanced up at him from between a thick set of long lashes. "Do you think you'll see her again if she feels ready in few months?"

Gary backed up at that question, looking too uncomfortable to answer, though that was answer enough for Mia. No way would he want to go out with her again after hearing what had happened. Too much baggage. Too much disgust.

Though she didn't blame him, she was relieved she didn't have worry about filling any expectations. But along with the relief came hurt. She backed away from the metal, gated wall separating them, not sure what to do . . . what to think. Piper had just told him her tragedy. It made her wonder. Had her roommate gone around to everyone and explained Mia's problems? Had she told Drew?

Shuddering, she wondered what Drew thought of her now. He hadn't mentioned his knowledge of her past either time they'd spoken on the phone since Piper had cut his hair. But then, Mia had been too busy on both occasions berating him to give him the opportunity.

Oh, God, she'd yelled at him, accusing him of being awful. And all this time, he might've known what she'd done to the one person she loved most in the world.

It was a sobering realization. She wondered what his initial response had been. Disgust? Loathing? Pity? She could handle the first two. It was exactly what had been plaguing her for three years. But pity? No, that was all wrong. Every time someone told her they were sorry about what happened, the guilt and blame slammed into her a hundred times stronger. It sliced into her and choked her with self-hatred and regret.

Irritated, yet relieved Piper had canceled her date for her, Mia drove home, consumed in misery. She wondered how often her roommate had butted in where she didn't belong for Mia's benefit. Suddenly annoyed, malevolence toward Piper grew for the first time in over three years.

Just as quickly, Mia shoved the aggravation aside. Piper was only trying to help, and Mia hated her for it? It was a good thing both Gary and Drew didn't want anything to do with her anymore. She didn't deserve to move on. She didn't need any kind of happiness. Not when she was such a mess.

CHAPTER TWELVE

The Lakeside Elementary end-of-the-school year concert took place in their gymnasium on the first Friday during their last month of classes.

Drew resituated himself in his metal folding chair for about the fiftieth time in the past minute. And his nephew unknowingly kicked him in the knee for about the hundredth time. He glanced over and scowled at the boy's mother while Felix continued to wiggle on her lap.

"How much longer?" he asked Mandy. She glanced briefly at her watch. The program hadn't even started yet and his butt was already numb.

"Five minutes," she announced.

"Where's Jeff again?" he asked. This wasn't fair. Why did he have to get stuck watching a few hundred off-tune kids sing " 'Til We Meet Again," when the father to two of them was off who knows where, getting to sit through business meetings. Lucky jerk.

Amanda sent him a dirty look, probably because he'd just reminded her of her husband's absence. "He said he had a meeting in Denver."

"He said," Drew repeated, noticing she hadn't worded it, "He's in Denver for a meeting."

Amanda glowered and then glanced at her son. Eyes softening, she brushed a few messed hairs off Felix's dark forehead.

Drew wanted to apologize for his mood, but then someone turned off a few rows of lights and piano music began. The concert was ahead of schedule, thank God.

As the curtains opened and a class full of kindergarteners dressed as sunflowers began to sing, he thought of Mia. Her call still bothered him.

He knew he should be relieved. Jeff wasn't cheating on his sister. But he hadn't told Amanda about the call. Something felt off about it.

Worried about Mia, he'd called five times before he gave up that avenue and drove over to her house, willing to even talk to her roommate again to see her. But she hadn't been home and neither had Piper. He knew he shouldn't despise Piper anymore, but he still tasted bitter repugnance when he thought of her. He wasn't sure if he'd ever get over the fact he thought she'd been ruining Mandy's marriage, not the way he'd gotten over fearing Mia was doing the same thing.

His sister elbowed him in the side and leaned close. "Lucy's class is next. She was almost in tears tonight when we put her dress on her and it was too small. I swear that girl sprouted up a foot overnight."

Drew glanced to his left to watch the way Amanda smiled in pride. She seemed so relaxed tonight as she focused on her children. He'd been worried she'd fall apart if Jeff ended up being unfaithful. But he realized now how he'd underestimated the power of motherhood. Merely watching a kid grow was enough to keep Mandy happy and satisfied.

Envious, he wondered if he'd ever experience that total contentment of being a parent. With Mia hating him as she seemed to, he wasn't too optimistic. Not that he blamed her for putting an end to their shaky start. Even though the Jeff/Piper thing ended up being a false alarm, it probably would've been too awkward between him and Mia to make a go of things. Amanda's disapproval — oh, and she would disapprove — would cause enough strain to scare anyone off.

Drew loved his sister to death, but she'd never kept it a secret when she didn't like one of his girlfriends. They usually gave him the typical Dear John the first time they met her. He should probably resent her for that, but he'd always been too relieved he didn't have to see that particular woman again . . . until Mia. He didn't like the thought of Mandy scaring Mia off.

One group of children shuffled offstage and the next entered. The music changed and Drew lifted his face, searching for his niece. As if reading his mind, Mandy said, "She's on the second row up, third from the left."

Drew narrowed his search to the second row and there she was, wearing a white dress that matched every other girl in her class. Lucy grinned and waved when she caught sight them. Enchanted, he offered a small wave in return.

"She's adorable," he said, thinking no other girl in her class shared her cuteness.

"You're biased," Amanda murmured, sounding amused. "But, yes, she definitely rates high on the adorable chart."

He rolled his eyes at her answer but didn't respond, except to slip from his chair and follow a dozen other dads to the edge of the stage to take pictures, though he doubted none of them toted a four thousand dollar camera to snap off a shot.

As he zoomed in and focused on Lucy, he thought about her mother. It was nice to be around Mandy without listening to her paranoia, without getting badgered about what information he'd discovered for her. He should probably be worried because of that fact. When they were younger and she stopped telling him not to do something, it was usually because she was about to strike and thump him in the shoulder. But this was relaxing . . . well, as relaxing as anyone could get when they were crammed into a gymnasium with three hundred other sets of parents.

The concert continued without mishap — except for the time a second-grade boy turned nervous and threw up in the hair of the girl standing in front of him. But to Drew, that all narrowed down to comic relief. After clicking a couple candid shots of both Lucy and Natalie, he returned to his seat to find Felix conked out on Amanda's lap with his head relaxed on her shoulder. His nephew looked so adorable, Drew took a picture of mother and son together.

Once the final song was over and the entire school came on stage to sing their grand finale, he shuffled behind Amanda to pick up her two daughters in their class-rooms where they waited. He snapped off a few more shots of Lucy and Natalie in their rooms and then he made all three children pose with their mother.

"Oh, that one was nice," he said after Lucy hugged Natalie in excitement over her big performance. "I might have to put it on display in my studio."

Amanda rolled her eyes, but wasn't able to hide her smile. "You already have too many of them in your studio."

"Well, if they'd just stop being so cute, I'd probably stop." With that, he clicked off another picture of Felix trying to pick up an older girl in Lucy's first-grade class.

"You're going to give me a set of proofs, right?" Amanda asked as she watched him work.

"Don't I always? I'll put them on a disk as soon as I get home."

She nodded in approval and then turned to her three children. "Say goodbye to Uncle Drew, guys. We need to get home and into the bath. It's past bedtime."

After receiving four different hugs from three different children, Drew waved his sister's family off and started home himself. But once he reached his quiet, echoing house, he felt even more forlorn than usual. There was nothing like a hoard of hundreds of school kids singing "Stand By Me" to remind him how alone he was.

He closeted himself in his office, going over each picture he'd taken on his print shop. Glad he grew up in the electronic age, he cut out the background in the picture of Felix draped over Amanda's shoulder and put them in the living room of Amanda and Jeff's house. Though he'd said he wanted to blow up the shot of Lucy and Natalie hugging, this is the one that drew him the most.

Working until a quarter after eleven, he packaged his photo card to send to Miller's Professional Imaging, who'd have his proofs back in record time. Then he turned off his computer and shuffled upstairs toward his bedroom. Five minutes later, he lay in bed with his arms propped behind his head as he stared up at his ceiling. But sleep didn't come. Wondering if Mia was still awake, he reached for his cell phone on his nightstand, unable to help himself. Earlier, he'd tried calling Mia from his cell, thinking he could surprise her into picking up the unfamiliar number. But she hadn't.

He pushed redial and waited. It rang once before he disconnected. Man, what was he doing?

She'd made it perfectly clear she didn't want anything to do with him. And if he hadn't caught that hint, she'd called again with her I-told-you-so call today, letting him know Piper was definitely not seeing his brother-in-law.

Sighing, he tossed the cell phone on his nightstand and rolled onto his side, not finding sleep until he brought up the memory of his non-date with Mia, teasing each other about their pizza preferences and then kissing at her car.

He murmured her name once before exhaustion overcame him.

Mia had just reached for the phone when it cut off in mid ring. Frowning at the oddity of that, she checked the caller id and read, "Incomplete Data." Dang. She gnawed on her lip a second longer.

For some reason, she knew it was Drew. But then she boiled that mind-set down to wishful thinking. He wouldn't call her again after the way she'd yelled at him and hung up. And she didn't want him to call either, though, oh God, she really did.

Tonight, especially after watching Gary recoil from the idea of dating her, after realizing Piper went around spreading her secret, after the guilt and pain that was still swarming her, she really needed a good, strong dose of Drew. She still had no idea what it was about him that made everything okay again. But it was something she could definitely get used to. Not that it mattered. She wasn't going to see him again.

She needed some cheering up for that reason too. It was depressing and ironic to think about how she'd just lost the one person who gave her hope.

Picking up the phone, she dialed him back until she remembered she wasn't even certain it had been Drew who called, so she slammed the phone down. It could've been Piper, one of Piper's friends, her parents, a die-hard telemarketer . . . even a wrong number.

Chances were, it hadn't been Drew.

She moped her way back to her bedroom and crawled under the covers. Falling into a fitful sleep, she woke a few hours later to hear Piper returning home for the evening, but her consciousness was so distorted, she would've sworn she heard double, because it sounding like two sets of footsteps tromping down the hall and disappearing into Piper's room. And it sounded like two voices talking. But she drifted back into dreamland so quickly, she probably just imagined everything.

■ ■ ■ ■

Drew was dead asleep when the call came. Not bothering to turn on a light or even open his eyes, he swung out an arm and fumbled in the dark until he found his cell.

" 'Lo."

"Drew, I need you."

The feminine voice made him crack open an eye. "Who's this?" he slurred out.

"It's Amanda," she hissed. "Your sister."

"Mandy?" He sat up, clicking on his bedside lamp and then rubbing at his tired eyes. "What time is it?"

"I don't know. After twelve. He's over there."

"Huh?" He reached out to turn his alarm clock around. Half past midnight. Dear God, this better be good. "What're you talking about?"

"Jeffrey. He's at her house. Right now."

Pausing in the middle of a stretch, Drew straightened. "He's not in Denver? How do you know?"

"Because he's at 410 South Elm, that's how I know. Dang it. His car's parked in their driveway. I drove by and saw it."

The breath rushed from his lungs. "What? When'd you do that?"

205

A million more questions swirled through him. Did Mia know? Wait. He knew that answer. Of course she knew. She had to know. But she'd told him —

"I went by when I was taking the kids home from the concert," Amanda answered. "I took the long way . . . past her place."

His jaw dropped. "You had the kids with you?"

"No," she muttered sarcastically. "I dropped them off on the corner and came back to pick them up after driving by. Yes, they were with me." She snorted.

"Did any of them see his car?"

She gasped. "I hadn't thought of that. But, no. If they'd seen anything, they would've said something."

"No, wait," Drew cut in, lifting a hand. Awareness was starting to soak in. "The concert was finished by eight-thirty. That was over three hours ago. Why are you calling now?"

"He told me he had a business trip." Amanda snorted, ignoring his question and beginning her own rant. "But I knew he was lying."

"Mandy," he ground out.

"I had the kids with me, Drew. I couldn't do anything then. But I can't take this anymore. I really need you to come stay with my children while I go get my husband. I can't just sit here, doing nothing, knowing he's over there . . . with her."

Drew blew out a breath. "Listen to me, Mandy. Don't go over there. I don't want you to see anything that's going to —"

"Drew —"

"If you're sure he's there, I'll get him. Okay? I will get him. Do not go over there."

He would, but he prayed his sister came to her senses and let this go for the night. What was done was done. Jeff was at Mia's house. She'd lied to him and Jeff had lied to Amanda and —

"You will?" Amanda asked in a hopeful voice. "Oh, thank you, Drew. I don't want him over there a second longer. I can't stand it."

He winced, realizing this was going to happen. "Of course I will," he answered, though he didn't want to go anywhere near Mia.

Had she purposely called earlier to mislead him because she knew Jeff was there? Had she finagled such a grand scheme because Jeff was seeing her . . . not Piper?

His throat burned as he pushed off his sheets and hurried out of bed. Jeff was at 410 South Elm, and he was either sleeping in Piper's bed or Mia's. In less than twenty minutes, he was going to find out the truth.

Anger, resentment, and hurt rushed through him as he stumbled toward the exit, gripping his keys and praying Mia hadn't purposely lied to him.

CHAPTER THIRTEEN

Mia had no idea how long someone had been knocking on her front door. She'd been dreaming of Lexie again, learning to walk.

Gasping awake, Mia sat up in bed and jumped when the hammering came again. She stumbled, hitting her knee on the bedpost as she fumbled for a robe, tying it around her waist. She could've sworn she'd woken earlier to Piper coming home, but that memory was like a foggy dream.

Her roommate had probably forgotten her house keys . . . again. Wiping her tired eyes and yawning, Mia hurried from the room, barefoot and not bothering to turn on a light as she felt her way through the dark to the front door.

Ready to berate Piper for forgetting her keys and waking her from her favorite dream, she threw open the door. "You really need to — Drew!" She blinked and stumbled a startled step back. "What're you doing here?"

Though it was dark and she could barely make him out from the streetlights, she could tell his jaw was hard and his eyes glacial. "I need to talk to Jeff," he bit out.

She blinked, still foggy from sleep, certain she'd just misheard him. "Excuse me?"

"My brother-in-law," he clarified with a growl, his voice growing louder with each word. "Jeffrey Alan Wright. His car is sitting right there in your driveway, Mia. So, either he's in here with your roommate, or he's in here with you. Either way, I'm going to talk to him."

Unable to stop herself, Mia leaned out to check the driveway. When she saw the foreign Charger sitting behind her Nissan, she gasped. "But it can't be. Piper said —"

"Then Piper lied." Drew didn't seem fazed by her shock. Continuing with his agenda, he stepped into the house and made to move around her.

She quickly dodged in front of him and set her hand against his chest. "What do you think you're doing? You can't just go back there and —"

"Oh, yes I can. My sister is sitting at home alone in her kitchen right now, bawling her eyes out. And it's his fault. His fault."

When she could only gape at him, he let out a sigh of frustration, his patience wearing out.

"Jeff," he bellowed, making Mia jolt.

"Drew!" she whispered in horrified alarm, already imagining the lights coming on in every house down the block with neighbors pouring from their front doors to see what the problem was.

"Jeffrey, you lousy brother-in-law," Drew continued to roar. "Get out here right now."

From the back of the house, there was a thump and then some cursing. Whirling from Drew, Mia gasped and set her hand over her mouth. Seconds later, a stranger she'd never met before appeared from the darkness of the hallway, wearing nothing but boxer shorts and black dress socks pulled halfway up his calves. He was probably in his late thirties, early forties and sported a healthy sized gut.

Seeing him, Mia shrank protectively against Drew who stood seething behind her.

"What in the world," the older man slurred out, tripping on an end table as he hurried into the living room. Squinting at Mia and Drew framed in the doorway, he jerked to a stop when he recognized the man behind her.

"Drew?"

Mia covered her mouth with both hands. She couldn't believe it. Drew's brother-in-law was in her house. Piper had indeed lied to her.

"Get your clothes on and go home to your wife," Drew growled. His voice was so menacing, Mia tensed as if bracing herself. But instead of shying away from him, she moved closer, seeking his protection and comfort.

"What — how — where's Amanda?" Jeff asked.

"She's waiting for you at home," Drew informed him coolly.

Drew's brother-in-law went still. "She knows?" he rasped unsteadily.

"Who do you think sent me here?" Drew bit out. "Now put some clothes on and go home."

Hurrying to comply, Jeff whirled around only to bump into Piper, finally arriving to see what all the commotion was about.

"Move," Jeff growled at her, taking her shoulders and physically setting her aside.

"What's going on?" she mumbled, rubbing at her eyes and yawning as he disappeared. Then she noticed Mia in the entrance with Drew.

Blinking a few times, she pointed and

mumbled, "Hey. What're you doing here?"

"I'm the brother to your boyfriend's wife," Drew told her.

Mia shivered, a little concerned what he might do to Piper. Piper froze and her mouth fell open. "Oh," she finally said, and then winced. "Oops."

"Yeah. Oops," Drew bit out stonily. He vibrated, and Mia unconsciously reached back and grappled for his hand. When he didn't pull away and actually returned the grip, squeezing her fingers, a jolt arrowed deep inside her.

It was nice knowing he needed her support. Satisfying.

"Did you know he was married?" he asked, making Piper shift weight and give a half-hearted shrug. "Did you know they had three kids together?"

Piper's hand was shaking as she lifted a few fingers to the corner of her eye. "He showed me pictures," she admitted on a whisper.

Drew's grasp on Mia's hand tightened painfully; she moved even closer, leaning fully against his chest.

"Do you know how much his wife loves him?" he pressed. "For twelve years, she's stood by his side, supporting him through college, raising his children, feeding and

213

clothing him without complaint. Does that not mean anything to you?"

Piper choked out a sob and whirled away, slamming her hand over her mouth and hurrying down the hall toward her room.

Every muscle in Drew's body seized as if he wanted to go after the adulteress. Mia spun around to face him, resting both her hands on his chest. She was so close she had to tilt her head back to see his face, shadowed as it was in the dim light.

"I'm so sorry," she whispered. "I had no idea he was here. Drew, please believe —"

He wrapped his hand lightly around her wrist and tenderly pulled her fingers from his chest. That he cared enough to be gentle affected her more than if he'd shoved her away.

His eyes slid to hers. "You already made it clear whose side you're on, Mia."

He took a step backward until he was standing outside the doorway, physically drawing the line between them.

Brows wrinkling to show his misery, he shook his head. "I have to go babysit now," he said, his voice cracking. Then he turned stiffly and strode off her steps heading for his truck.

Mia just stood there dumbly, and watched him drive away.

Hearing footsteps behind her, she turned to find Jeffrey Wright, shirttails hanging loose from his pants, tucking a wallet into his back pocket as he hurried into the front room. He faltered when he saw her. They both paused, neither speaking a word as they studied each other. Then Mia stepped back, clearing the exit for him. He nodded a brief thanks and hurried out the door.

She closed it behind him, locking and bolting it. Then she pressed her face to the wooden panel. Her hand came up and fisted against the door. She pounded once for the injustice of it all.

Poor Drew, she thought. *Poor Drew's sister.* Amanda had known all along something wasn't right, and Mia had been reluctant to do anything about it.

This was Piper's fault, she decided. Piper and Drew's brother-in-law. Because of them, she wasn't going to see Drew again, and she'd probably digress further into herself. Why would Piper date a married man then lie about breaking up with him? It made no sense.

She found Piper in her room, sitting on an unmade bed with her head bowed and her hands fisted in her lap.

"Piper?"

Her roommate lifted her face. The light

215

from the hall beaming into the dark room immediately picked up the shine of tears on her cheeks.

"He said he was going to leave her," she rasped, sniffing and wiping at her eyes.

Mia had to force herself not to roll her eyes. She moved into the room and sat gingerly next to Piper.

"He said he'd already gone to the lawyer and filed for a divorce. But he lied to me, didn't he?"

Mia nodded softly. "Yeah, I think so."

"He spent hours telling me about his kids, showing me pictures and making me fall in love with them. I was actually preparing myself to be a stepmother."

"I'm so sorry." Mia reached for her friend's hand.

Piper lifted her face. "I didn't know he was related to your Drew."

Swallowing, Mia gave a miserable nod.

"If you want, I'll go talk to him — Drew, that is. Jeff can go to the devil for all I care. But I'll apologize to your Drew if you want. You've done so much better with him around. You —"

"No," Mia said, frowning. "Don't."

"But," Piper frowned. "You like him. After three years of seeing you so miserable, it was like . . . It was amazing to see you smile again. He makes you smile, Mia. I'll do anything to get the old you back. It makes me sick to think my getting involved with a married man came between you and your first chance at happiness. I'll talk to him. I'll tell him you didn't know. I'll do anything —"

"Piper," Mia cut in squeezing her grip on the other woman's hand. "Thank you, but . . . no more lies. Besides, I'd like to try talking to him myself."

"Make sure he realizes you didn't know what I was doing. That I lied to you."

Mia shook her head. "It shouldn't matter if I knew or not. You're my friend. I have a right to keep your affairs secret if I want to."

Her roommate cringed. "No pun intended," she muttered. After she sniffed and wiped at her wet eyes, she looked sadly at Mia. "Why does life have to be so painful?"

Sighing, Mia leaned over to rest her head on Piper's shoulder. "We wouldn't know what happiness was if we didn't have something bad to compare it to."

A lifetime of happy moments washed through her. Winning the spelling contest in the second grade, graduating high school and college, hearing a proposal from Ryan, holding her newborn baby girl and raising

217

her for three months, turning from her flowerbed and seeing Drew for the first time, kissing Drew. Those moments wouldn't have been so outstanding if she'd never known pain and sorrow.

"I have a confession," she admitted, lifted her face and glancing hesitantly at Piper. Biting her bottom lip, she said, "I knew Drew suspected you were . . . dating his brother-in-law."

Her roommate's eyes widened. "What? But —"

"His sister saw the credit card bill he used to buy your roses."

Mouth falling open, Piper gasped, "Okay, that explains a few things. Drew acted . . . so strange when I was talking about my roses with him. He —" She covered her mouth and gaped at Mia with large eyes. "He hurried out the salon right after he asked about them. And he looked upset. I thought . . . I assumed he felt bad because he hadn't thought of buying you flowers. I never — Oh, wow. How long have you known?"

Anger and accusations were absent from her question. She merely sounded curious as if she was trying to fit all the pieces together.

"Honestly, Piper," Mia started. "Why

aren't you livid? I kept something important from you."

"I have no reason to be mad," Piper said. She patted Mia's hand. "I'm the last person on earth worthy to cast blame at anyone about keeping secrets. I mean, look at me. I was dating a married man and kept it from my best friend."

"Why were you?" Mia blurted out, slapping a hand over her mouth. "Never mind," she quickly added. "It's none of my business."

"No, it's okay," Piper assured. "I want to talk about it. I . . . I've been incredibly stupid. But he was so different. Established for one, not like every other immature idiot who thought he was some kind of stud."

"But I'm sure there are plenty of single older men out there, Piper. If that's what —"

"I know," her friend interrupted. "But they're all so insecure. J was different because he had this charismatic confidence. I guess he could be that way, though, because he was so sure he could get a woman . . . he already had one. But at the time, I was grateful for such a refreshing change of pace."

Thinking over Piper's words, Mia grew grateful herself. She was grateful Piper hadn't met Drew before she had, otherwise, she probably would've dropped her older, married Jeff and gone after his younger, better-looking brother-in-law. Drew held a certain maturity about him without the added age. And he hadn't possessed any qualms about pursuing Mia, though there were many things that should've deterred him.

Piper reached for Mia's hand. "Oh, Mi Mi, I've caused such a mess. Do you think Drew's sister will be okay? From listening to J, I thought their marriage was over. I thought she didn't love him. But Drew made it sound —"

"Don't think about it," Mia advised. "Just . . . try to stick with single men from now on. Okay?"

Piper nodded. "You have my word."

CHAPTER FOURTEEN

The longest night of Drew's life started with a school concert and ended with him sleeping on his sister's short, flowered loveseat.

He followed Jeff home. When he eased into the back kitchen door from the garage, using his key, he could tell his sister and her husband hadn't started fighting yet. Relieved, he hurried through the house to find Amanda and Jeff in the living room. She stood on one side, her arms tightly crossed over her chest. Jeff huddled by the front door, looking shell-shocked.

When Drew burst into the room, they both whirled to gape at him.

Amanda recovered first. "What're you doing here?"

Lifting both hands, he started, "Both of you, don't say anything to each other yet. Okay? Just . . . go somewhere else. Go to my place. I'll stay here with the kids. Just don't start fighting here. You don't want to scare the children. Especially Natalie. She'll understand too much."

"Okay," Amanda said. She rubbed at her arms as if she was freezing. "Okay," she said again, more jittery-acting than he'd ever seen her. "That's a good idea." She started for that door, past Drew.

He reached for her arm to give it an encouraging pat as she passed, but she paused and gave him a full hug in return, holding him hard and burying her face in his shoulder. He cupped her head and kissed her hair. She shuddered and sobbed out a hiccup-type moan.

Stroking her hair, he quietly murmured, "Shh. It'll be okay. It'll be okay," though he had no idea how. Could anything ever be okay again?

Amanda found courage from his words though. She straightened, stared him in the eye for a good five seconds. Then she managed a watery smile. Nodding, she patted his cheek lovingly and started from the room without glancing at her husband.

Once she was gone, Drew shifted his gaze to Jeff. At least the man looked suitably guilty and apologetic.

"You guys can ride over there separately," he said.

Though he'd never given his brother-in-law a command before, it didn't come out timid or even feel awkward. He was actually ready and willing to give Jeff a few more commands, telling him where to go and how to get there. But this wasn't the time. He was only here to act as the babysitter, not get in the middle of a married couple's dispute. So, he held his tongue.

Jeff nodded in response to Drew's suggestion. As if wanting to give his wife a head start, he waited until they heard Mandy's Honda start before he made a move toward the door. Then he bowed his head and started out. Drew stepped aside to give him more room to pass, but Jeff paused next to him.

He reached for Drew's shoulder as he said, "Thank you, Drew."

But Drew stepped back before his brother-in-law could make contact. He had no sympathy for this man. No "it'll be okays" or heartfelt hugs for Jeffrey.

Jeff waited a frozen moment before dropping his hand. Then he nodded in understanding before he ducked his head and fled.

Finally deflating, Drew sagged against the door and stayed there until he heard Jeff's car start as well. Then he slumped toward the loveseat and collapsed. He was tired, but sleep didn't come. Too many thoughts raced through his mind to allow him rest. He wondered what Amanda and Jeff were talking about. He pictured Mia's shock as she glanced outside and caught sight of Jeff's car in her driveway. He worried how his nieces and nephew would react if he was still here in the morning when they woke.

Since they were his main priority at the moment, he eased down the hall toward their rooms, hoping their parents hadn't done anything to wake them before he'd arrived.

They were still dead asleep, thank God. Felix lay sprawled out on his back, totally open and relaxed with his arms and legs hogging the whole bed. Lucy curled into a ball and looked like a kitten nestled among the sheets. Natalie stirred restlessly when he checked on her. She'd scissor-kicked her sheets half off. He took the edge and pulled them back over her.

Once he returned to the living room, he stood in the center of the floor and rubbed at the center of his forehead, wishing he were somewhere else, wishing this wasn't happening.

Neither wishes were granted, so he settled himself once again on the loveseat. It was warm, so he kicked off his shoes and removed the throw blanket Amanda had draped over the back rest. He lay down with his feet hanging off the end and stared across the dark room, wishing he could do something a little more productive to help Amanda, like beat her lying, cheating husband to a pulp. But watching her kids was the most helpful he could be, so he stayed put, drifting in and out of sleep, waking to check the clock on the wall every few hours or wander through the house, making sure Natalie, Lucy and Felix were okay.

He was still conscious when Amanda returned home alone at five in the morning. When he heard the garage door open, he sat up, yawning. His muscles were sore and cramped. Ignoring his shoes, he padded through the house to meet Amanda in the kitchen.

Her face was dry but her eyes were red and swollen. There was no sound of Jeff's Charger pulling into the drive.

Drew breathed out a curse, imagining the worst. Amanda burst into tears, and he ran his hands through his hair, remaining frozen, telling himself not to ask. If she needed to talk about it, he'd be here, but he wasn't going to force her to open up if she didn't want to. She was upset enough as it was.

"We're getting a divorce," she sobbed.

As the truth repeated itself through his head, a burning heat washed over him and his face flamed with emotion. He glanced away from his sister, blinking rapidly. Though it had been twenty-one years since his mother had walked out and his dad had told them she wasn't coming back, he still remembered the moment clearly. And it hadn't hurt like this. But he hadn't been so aware back then. Plus he'd known Jeff longer than he'd known his mother and formed a stronger bond.

Refusing to lose it in front of his sister who needed him to stay strong, he sniffed his misery back in and quietly asked, "Where is he now?"

She shrugged. "Who knows. Maybe he went back to the hotel he's been staying in while he was pretending to be in Denver. Maybe he's at her house. Who cares?"

"Do you," he gulped in a breath. "Do you want to talk about it?"

"Oh, Drew," she wailed stumbling across the kitchen in his direction. "It was so awful."

Grateful he could finally do something, he pulled her into a hug and held her close, glad she couldn't see his face now, because he definitely had tears in his eyes.

"He made it out to be my fault. I never

talked to him about his job, never gave him the physical relationship he needed. I wasn't good enough of a wife." She lifted her face, looking devastated. "Do you think I was a bad wife?"

He shook his head violently. He would've denied it even if he had thought so, but he could remember so many times she'd given up things for Jeff. She'd raised Jeff's children with almost no help from him. She'd stayed home and cooked and cleaned when she could've gone out. She'd been the perfect housewife, even though she'd worked forty hours a week at the bank. She'd worked so hard.

"Listen to me," he growled, clutching her face in his hands. "He was just caught at his mistress's house. He's going to say anything right now to keep the blame off him. He's going to make any kind of excuse he can. No one likes to admit they're one hundred percent to blame."

"But I never —"

"If he was that miserable, he could've told you about it a long time ago instead of finding someone else. Mandy, he was wrong."

A new string of tears started. Worried he'd only made the matter worse, he sat her at a chair at the table and hurried to the stove to make her a kettle of hot tea. Still remembering she liked to brew tea when she was upset, he dipped a teabag into a mug of hot water once it was ready, spooned in a teaspoon of sugar and placed it in front of her.

She reached out immediately and wrapped her hands around the cup. He opened his mouth to warn her it was hot and to wait a minute before she took a drink. But then he realized she just wanted to hold the mug, like she was cold and needed some warmth and comfort.

"How're the kids?" she asked.

"They slept the entire night and are still in bed."

She nodded. "Good."

He caught sight of a box of Kleenex and snatched it up, bringing it to the table as he sat across from her. He passed her a single sheet and she wordlessly used it to dab at her wet cheeks.

"Thank goodness they still think he's in Denver. I don't know what I'm going to do when it's time they think he should come home."

Felix and Lucy were more like he had been, Drew realized. They wouldn't be so concerned about their father's absence. Where he'd been a sister's boy, they were momma's babies and wouldn't miss Jeff.

Natalie, on the other hand, would hurt.

"We'll have to . . . to . . . work out a custody arrangement," Mandy admitted, fresh tears welling.

Drew pulled another tissue from the box and handed it over. She took it gratefully and blew her nose.

"What all happened tonight?" he finally asked.

"We fought mostly," she admitted. "I blamed him, and he blamed me. And then he said, 'I can't live like this anymore.' And I was like, 'live like what?' I had no idea he'd been so miserable, Drew. If he was that dissatisfied why didn't he come to me? Why didn't he tell me? I just don't understand."

Not sure how to respond, Drew sat there, ready with another Kleenex.

"All I can remember is back when we were dating and he took me out to the park in the middle of the night and sang the Boston song, *Amanda,* to me. It was so sweet. I think I fell in love with him right then." Her eyes were so tear-stained they seemed to float in their sockets. "What went wrong?"

He shook his head, unable to answer. "I don't know, Sis. I don't know."

It was almost noon by the time Drew made it home. He'd already called his one appointment scheduled for the day and cancelled. Every muscle in his body screamed from exhaustion. He ignored them, tramping through his house to the back kitchen.

He opened the fridge and yanked out a soda, crushing the aluminum can in his fist when he was done drinking.

He'd spent a majority of the morning with the kids in order to give Amanda some time alone. Even his brain was worn out. He plopped onto his kitchen stool located at the end of the cabinets and just sat there.

The world hadn't come to an end, but it was definitely pausing. One era had ended, and the next had yet to start. Drew rested his elbows on the counter, thinking what he should do next. As he contemplated, there came a knock at his door.

Thinking Amanda still needed him to watch her children, he slid off the stool and hurried toward the front room.

But it wasn't Amanda and her three children.

It was Jeff.

Drew pulled up short, his insides shutting down. Pain and anger roared through him.

His brother-in-law lifted his face. "Can I come in?"

He'd known this man since he was fourteen. Jeff wasn't just that guy married to his sister. Jeff was a brother.

"Were you ever faithful to her?" he asked, gritting his teeth when his voice broke.

Jeffrey stiffened. "I'm not going to talk about my relationship with Amanda to you."

And thank God for that. Drew had never understood their marriage. But he hadn't really wanted to either. They were his family. As long as they stayed that way, he didn't care what kind of odd bond they shared.

"Then what're you doing here?"

Jeff seemed to wilt before him. "It's the kids," he said, glancing down at his hands. "I'm worried about them."

Drew shrugged. He'd seen the man's kids minutes ago. They looked fine to him. Even Natalie hadn't suspected anything. Probably because they were used to Daddy being gone on trips and didn't yet realize he wasn't coming back this time.

"What about them?" he asked.

"Drew. Let me in." Jeff shuffled uncomfortably. "You wouldn't even have this place if I hadn't let Amanda give it to you."

Drew froze. That was true, and it was a low blow.

"I don't owe you anything," he hissed. "If you had a problem with me living here, you should've said something a long time ago. You can have it back if it's that important to you."

Jeff sighed, letting Drew know he'd been bluffing. "I don't want your stupid house," he mumbled. "I just want to talk to you."

"About the kids?"

"Yes!"

"You don't want to stay here for a while?"

Jeff's head came up and he stared at Drew in surprise. "They shouldn't have to go through this," he finally muttered.

Drew snorted incredulously. "If you were so concerned about how it would affect them then maybe you shouldn't have messed up your marriage."

Glancing away guiltily, Jeff mumbled, "I know your parents' divorce bothered her. She always talked about how that wasn't going to happen to her children."

Drew shuddered. "So why are you making it happen to them?"

"You don't understand what it's like," Jeff groaned. He spun away and paced the length of the porch. When he returned, he only looked more agitated. "When I was in school, I was it, you know. The most-popular, best-looking, biggest athlete."

Folding his arms to show how unimpressed he was, Drew leaned against the door frame. "So?"

"So? Now, I'm nothing. Some middle-class worker in some middle-class world, living some middle-class life. When I met Piper . . ."

Shuddering, Drew narrowed his eyes, hating the animated way Jeff said her name. He waited for Jeff to continue but was glad when he didn't.

"You want to know something," he responded. "I know one woman and three small children who would think you're amazing if you just spent some time with them once in while. You might not be anything to the world, but you were the world to them. Were," he repeated cruelly. "Not anymore."

Jeff's jaw dropped as if he'd never realized that fact before. He blinked repeatedly. Then he murmured, "They always adored Amanda more than they did me."

"Maybe because Amanda is a parent to them," Drew suggested. "You're just that guy that lives in their house and yells at them when they get in his way. You could be so much more if you'd just stop sleeping with every hairdresser that smiles at you and spend that time with your family."

Clearly taken aback, Jeff asked, "How did you know she works as a —"

"I know a lot more than you think. Unlike you, I pay attention when Mandy talks to

233

me." His brother-in-law remained quiet. "She put all her energy into those kids because she's been forced to practically raise them by herself. If you would've helped her out and taken on half the duties, she would've had more time for you."

"Whoa," Jeff gasped. "You really do know a lot."

Nodding in agreement, Drew said, "Your children will be just fine without you. They always have been."

Turning away, Jeff clutched his head and let out an anguished moan. "I messed up," he confessed.

Drew snorted. "Gee, you think?"

"What do I do? How do I fix this?"

Sounding like a broken record, because he'd already repeated these exact same words to Mandy, he said, "I don't know." He didn't mention how he didn't think Jeff could fix anything, but he definitely thought it.

"Thank you, Drew," his brother-in-law murmured. "You made me realize a few things I hadn't understood before."

Wanting to be nasty and tell him it was about time he pulled his head out of the sand, Drew remained quiet.

"I'll see you later," Jeff said. He turned and started for his charger.

Wondering if he really would see Jeff ever again, Drew watched him go.

CHAPTER FIFTEEN

Mia turned into Harper Studio's driveway, wondering for the thousandth time if coming here was a huge mistake. She had to be the last person Drew wanted to talk to. But she couldn't stay away.

He'd been so upset when he'd come for his sister's husband. She worried how he was taking everything.

She'd stayed away for almost a week, but the worry ate at her, so she waited a few hours longer, until she was sure he had to be off work for the evening and she started over, anxiety spiking from head to toe.

The front door was open, just like the first time she had visited, letting a draft float through his screen. She pushed the doorbell and took a cautious step back.

He must've been cooking because he appeared with a greasy spatula in hand.

"Hi," she said, and took another step back, holding her breath.

His step faltered. "Mia?"

The wavering smile she sent wasn't so encouraging, but she tried anyway. "May I come in?"

His mouth opened, but his didn't immediately speak, the internal debate clear in his eyes.

Before he could answer, a beeping came from the back of his house and he jumped. So did she.

"Hold on," he told her, turning on his heel and hurrying toward the kitchen timer.

As soon as he disappeared, she opened the door and stepped into the front room. Figuring that was as bold as she could get, she wandered along the walls, noticing he'd hung new pictures. The 20 × 24 framed portrait of Amanda cradling a sleeping boy on her shoulder caught her attention. This must be his nephew. She lifted her finger to touch the boy's cheek through the glass.

He was precious. As hard as he slept against his mother, she could tell he was a wild one, full of life and always raring to go. Just like Lexie had been. She'd be a couple of years younger than him if she was alive.

Footsteps approaching behind her told Mia that Drew had taken care of whatever had needed his attention in the kitchen. She turned as he rounded the corner and pulled to a startled stop.

"Oh," he said when he realized she'd come in.

Mia waited a heartbeat for him to explode and kick her out. When he didn't, she took a breath to bolster her courage. "How's your sister?"

He shot her a bitter look. "She's getting a divorce," he looked evilly pleased to report. "They've already set up custody, and this is her kids' first weekend with their father."

"Oh." She stared down at her clasped hand. Did divorces move so fast?

"How's your roommate," he asked with a sneer.

Ignoring his tone, she said, "She's upset because . . . your brother-in-law dumped her."

He made a humming sound in his throat. "I'd say I'm sorry to hear that. But . . ."

"No," she assured him. "There's no reason for you to lie."

"So, why are you here," he asked softly. "Wanted to make sure Amanda and Jeff were truly over before you encouraged your friend to run after him?"

She braced herself against his ugly tone. "No," she answered. "I came to see how you were doing."

He shifted uncomfortably, glancing away

from her. "I'm not the one getting a divorce," he mumbled. "There's no reason to worry about me."

"But . . ." She licked her lips and blew out a breath. He looked miserable; she told herself not to give up yet. "You lost a brother," she argued. "I'm sure your sister had been married awhile. Weren't you even a little close to her husband?"

He glanced at her with a sharp, accusing frown. But a second later, his shoulder slumped and he looked away again.

"Yeah," he finally admitted. "It feels like I lost a brother. I don't have a huge family as it is, and with him out of it now, a big percent just . . ." He shook his head. "I know I shouldn't be that upset. Amanda's going through so much more than I am. This is her husband, the father of her children. I should be there for her and stay strong, but . . ."

"It hurts," Mia whispered.

He closed his eyes and hissed out a breath. "Why am I telling you this?" His voice was sharp as he continued.

"Because we connect."

He snorted, opening his gaze to send her a frown. "We connect? I don't think so. I think it's more like I tell you everything and you keep secrets. I even had to hear from your roommate you were suffering from some kind of survivor's guilt. And I don't even know who died that was so important to you."

Mia froze. "She . . . she didn't tell you who?"

He shook his head.

"Do you want to know?" As soon as the question left her lips, she regretted it. She'd never really told the entire story to anyone before. Piper had explained her situation to people down here. And at home, everyone just knew.

But when Drew whispered, "Yes, I want to know," she shivered, apprehensive.

Swallowing like she was trying to gag down a chicken bone, Mia said, "Can we sit down somewhere for this story?"

"Is it that bad?"

Closing her eyes, she nodded. "Yes." Her voice was hoarse.

He drew near, and she almost sobbed when his fingers lightly touched her arm. "You don't have to tell me," he assured.

She opened her eyes. "Yes, I think I do."

Nodding, he took her hand. After closing the main door and locking it, he led her through his studio and into a back sitting room with a couch, two chairs, and a flat-screen television. She could immediately tell this was his living space by the relaxed aura. Rugs and more informal pictures decorated the walls, while a pair of shoes lay forgotten on a rug by the couch.

She glanced down and noticed his feet were bare. For some reason, that made her more nervous. This was going to be too intimate, too cozy. She was going to flip out on him and —

"Okay," he said, motioning toward all the cushions she could sit on.

After choosing the couch, she watched him settle into a chair across from her. It was impossible to tell if he just couldn't stand sitting any closer than that or if he wanted to give her space, but she appreciated the space . . . and the time as he remained quiet, letting her gather her thoughts.

She blew out a breath. "I'm going to tell you a story," she started. "It's pretty long and you'll probably wonder why I'm telling it, but . . . it all comes back to now. It explains my friendship with Piper, why I am the way I am, and why I'm even bothering to come here today, hoping to get your forgiveness." Looking baffled but curious, he settled back into his chair, getting comfortable. "I'm listening."

Great. Here went nothing.

"When I was twenty-four, I met this guy named Ryan."

Drew immediately shifted in his chair, already looking uncomfortable.

"We dated for about five months before I got pregnant."

Perking to attention, Drew sat up and blinked, not expecting to hear that twist in the story.

"I liked Ryan," she told him. "I mean, sure. We'd gotten serious enough to sleep together. But our relationship was nowhere near the settling-down stage, and becoming parents was the last thing we were planning at that time in our lives. To say the least, this was an unexpected surprise."

Drew nodded adamantly, agreeing with her.

"But we both decided we wanted the baby, and we tried to make a go of it. He proposed the day our daughter Alexis was born."

Confusion reigned in his features. "But where —"

Mia held up a hand, stopping him from asking any question she wasn't ready to answer yet. When he nodded and sat back, she took another moment to settle her racing heart.

"Life was so hectic those days," she murmured. "Suddenly I was a new mother, trying to plan a wedding, and then there was this precious little bundle of joy in my life." Eyes filling with tears, she smiled at Drew and said, "She was so wonderful. So perfect. I called her Lexie."

He visibly swallowed; his face drained of color.

Mia drew in a deep breath. "She was only three months old when it happened. I was exhausted all the time. Tired from the wedding plans, tired from taking care of Lexie, tired from work. I was still working part time, a night shift to help with the money. It seemed to drain the last of my energy. I didn't want to get up every time she woke. It was so much easier to bring her to bed with me."

"Oh no," he whispered, horror prevalent on his features; he could probably tell exactly where her story was headed. He rubbed at the back of his neck, showing his unease.

"I had a couple of pillows set up between the mattress and the wall, so she wouldn't roll over and hit her head or something, you know."

His nodded, fisting his hand against his mouth. His eyes were wide over his white knuckles.

But Mia couldn't stop talking. The words spilled out of her. "But she didn't hit the wall," her voice was hollow as she spoke. "She rolled under the pillow somehow and got stuck between the cushion and the mattress. It suffocated her to death."

Drew made a sound of regret and pain. She noticed his fingers were shaking and his knee was bobbing as he tried to contain his dread.

"I'd taken Infant CPR classes before she was born. I was actually prepared for this. But it was already too late. She'd probably been gone hours by the time I woke up."

He shook his head as if that would make her words untrue.

"What's worse," she continued, her voice going hoarse. "I couldn't even tell people it was SIDS. It wasn't SIDS. I'd flat out suffocated my baby."

"No." Drew shot off his chair, falling to his knees and crawling to her until he was setting his hands heavily on her legs. "Mia, you didn't —"

"I know," she said softly. "I've been through enough therapy and counseling to admit it was merely an accident. A very tragic, unfortunate accident."

"But you still feel guilty," he said. "I know I would."

"I was her mother. I was the one who was supposed to keep her safe, not put her in danger."

Drew took her limp hands from her lap and pulled them to his mouth kissing her fingers. "What about Ryan?"

Her gaze slid to her fingers still wet from his mouth. "He blamed me too."

"He what?" His face filled with hot anger. It warmed her to see him insulted on her behalf.

"He told me he didn't, of course. But he'd never touch me. I needed his comfort and understanding more than anything, and he needed the same from me. We were just too broken to help each other. We ended the engagement about a month after the funeral."

"I'm sorry," Drew whispered, keeping her hand pressed against his mouth in a tight grip.

Mia smiled sadly. "I want you to know, I didn't tell you this to get you to forgive me out of sympathy."

He shook his head. "There's nothing to forgive. You never did anything wrong."

"But you were so mad at me last week . . . and today."

He sighed. "I was just mad. Mad at Jeff, mad at your roommate, mad mostly for

Amanda's sake. I always knew you'd protect your friend, no matter what. It was never fair of me to ask you not to."

"She's been so good to me," Mia agreed. "About a year ago, I was so depressed, I . . ." She shook her head, not wanting to go there. "Anyway, my family called Piper. She'd been my closest friend since grade school. I used to be a lot like her." Grinning, she glanced down at Drew, who still sat perched on his knees on the floor before her. "I was outgoing and . . . well, maybe I wasn't as vivacious at Piper, but I could hold my own."

Drew sent her a soft smile and pecked a kiss to her knuckles. "I bet you did."

She reached out. Drew froze, only his eyes tracked the movement of her fingers. When she made contact with his hair, he closed his lashes and let out a breath. Sifting gently through the dark, curly locks, she eased and her stiff shoulders relaxed. "I would've been able to catch you a long time ago," she said.

He opened his eyes and lifted his gaze. Sounding amused, he admitted, "You already did."

Her hand glided down the side of his head until she had her palm on his neck, just under his ear where his steady heartbeat thumped against the pads of her fingers. It was strong and so alive.

"I mean, we could've probably been together by now. I wouldn't have freaked out every time you tried to touch me."

"Do you?" he asked quietly, his eyelids half closed and his smile lazy as if her touch was putting him to sleep. "I never noticed you freaking out."

"Liar."

He grinned, guilty. "It's never bothered me," he assured. "I swear. Going slow isn't a problem. We can go as slow as you want. Just as long as you still want to go there with me."

"I do," she said. "That's why I'm here. When I first turned around and saw you standing on my sidewalk, I knew. I haven't been able to . . . live properly for three years now. I've been going to a counselor, working through the stages of grief. But I haven't dated, haven't even talked to men I might want to date. I've been too afraid I might end up happy. That was my biggest fear of all. That last step . . . accepting I was still alive. But then I saw you, and something just clicked. I don't know what it was, but after about two minutes in your company, I knew I wanted you to be the one to make me happy again, to make me smile."

She bit her lip. "Am I scaring you off yet?

Heaping all these expectations on you?"

He shook his head. "Not yet. You're making me want to meet them all, though."

Relief shimmering through her, Mia grinned. "That's why I came here today. Because, so far, you've been the only person who made me want to get past my daughter's death."

He blew out a breath. "Wow." He shook his head. "Okay, now that's a little intimidating."

Eyes widening, Mia tried to pull her hand from his, but he tightened his grip.

"Doesn't mean I don't want to try, though." He stared into her eyes until his shoulders loosened and the features on his face softened. Then he leaned toward her.

She tipped her head down to meet him, and their lips brushed, like two cars passing on a street, their side mirrors barely skimming each other.

Mia's eyes fluttered open. "Is that all?" she asked, trying to hide the disappointment because her body was yearning for a little more contact.

The skin around his eyes crinkled. "Not even close," he answered and pressed his mouth to hers.

His fingers crept up the back of her neck and into her hair, cupping her head as he slanted his lips.

She gasped at the sensation. "Drew."

"I'm right here."

"Hold onto me before I float away."

He seemed more than happy to wrap his arms around her and press close.

He kissed her and her mind raced. Guilt consumed her: guilt for wanting to continue, and guilt for wanting to stop him from making her feel too good. Everything she did felt wrong. Feeling this sensational had to be wrong.

She broke away from him with a gasp. "I can't do this. I'm sorry, Drew. I can't —"

"No, shh," he cut in, cupping her face in his hands. "It's okay. You don't have to do anything." He leaned forward and kissed her forehead. "It's okay," he murmured again. Then he pulled back just enough to hover over her. "We won't do anything else."

"But I want to," she sobbed. Tears tracked down her cheeks. "I want to so bad. Then again, I don't want to either. I just can't move on."

Lifting her face, she showed her anxious expression. "What if Lexie's up in Heaven right now, looking down on me and seeing me like this? What if she thinks I've forgotten about her, that I don't care if she's gone or not? What if she thinks my time with her never meant anything? If I'm so blasé about moving on that I'll just go off and live happily ever after with the first guy who —"

"Mia." He took her arms. When she shook her head, he pulled her against him and hugged her hard. She remained stiff in his arms even as she buried her face in his chest.

"I just can't let go," she whispered.

"You're not letting her go," he assured. "You're . . . you're reassuring her."

"What?" She lifted her face and he reached out to brush away the wet tracks down her cheeks.

"If she's up there in Heaven, looking down on you, I'd say she's worried right about now."

"Because I'm with you?" she asked, looking worried.

He shook his head. "Because you're so sad." Pressing his forehead against her, he murmured, "Your daughter loved you, Mia. She would hate to see you upset like this. She would hate to see you miserable."

"I don't want to hurt anymore," she admitted weakly, sagging against him and letting him support her weight. He did, gladly.

"I know," he said, wiping her hair out of her eyes. "I know, baby."

When he sniffed, she lifted her face in

surprise. "You're crying."

Glancing away uneasily, he said, "So are you."

"But —"

"I don't like seeing you suffer like this," he admitted. "I wish I could do something — say something — to help you. I mean, if I thought stepping back and letting you go would honestly make you happier, I'd do it in a heartbeat. I'd back away from you. But I don't know anyone else that needs to be happy as much as you do. You don't have to feel guilty about being with me. I bet Lexie is probably thinking it's about time you started looking after yourself again."

Licking her lips, Mia said, "If . . . if I said okay, let's try this, would you . . . I mean, would you stop at any time. Even if we were —"

"Mia, it's okay," he said. "We don't have to do anything. You're not ready —"

"But I am." She ground her teeth because she was so frustrated. "I want to be ready so bad, Drew. I just want the pain to stop."

"It will," he assured her. "Someday, it'll get better. Might take a while though."

It already felt like it had taken forever.

"You don't ever have to worry about this kind of stuff between us. We can always stop . . . any time you need to. I don't want

251

you to feel any kind of pressure."

Whether he wanted it or not, she was already pressured. Her heart wanted everything with him and her head was freaking out over things she shouldn't even be thinking about.

Looking up at him, she touched his face and asked, "Would you keep going if I asked you to?"

His smile was genuine. Pressing his forehead to hers, he chuckled. "I think that answer's obvious. Whenever you're ready, I'm definitely your guy."

Tears clogged her lashes and she realized how much she loved him.

CHAPTER SIXTEEN

Drew woke warm and content. And starving. After tugging on a shirt and some shorts, he padded barefoot down the stairs and through a few parlors toward the kitchen. But in his office area, he heard the answering machine beep on his business line.

Curious as to who'd called so late last night — so late he'd been too tired to come downstairs and answer his phone — he paused and pushed play.

"Drew," a familiar female voice started, sounding concerned. "This is Piper. Piper Holliday. It's after midnight and Mia isn't home yet. She's been really quiet the past few days, and I'm worried about her. She's not by chance over there . . . is she?"

The message clicked off and he quickly reached forward to erase Jeff's mistress's voice from his phone. Since the call had been about Mia, he picked up his receiver and dialed her back. Piper answered drowsily, five rings later. " 'Lo."

"Mia's fine," he said. "You don't have to worry about her."

There was silence a moment and then she seemed to wake up again. "Oh . . ." she mumbled. Then, "Right. I know. I drove by your house last night and saw her car in the drive."

He pulled straight. "You drove by my house?"

"Uh huh. I was worried about Mia. The address was on your business card right below the phone number, so I decided to make sure she was okay."

Gritting his teeth, he growled, "Don't ever come to my house again. Or call here either. My sister visits a lot. I won't have you bothering her."

She didn't say anything at first. Then her irritated voice asked, "What? And you dating Mia won't bother her? It won't remind her what her husband did?"

He glanced guiltily toward the stairs. He still hadn't figured out how he wanted to deal with the problem yet. "That's not your concern," he muttered and hung up.

Closing his eyes and blowing a worried breath, he ran his fingers through his hair and straightened slowly. After one last troubled glance toward the stairs, he started for the kitchen. Cooking was always a good way to keep his mind off certain things. He decided breakfast in bed would be a nice treat for his house guest. He'd just removed the OJ from the freezer and the eggs from the fridge when he heard his front door open.

Thinking Mia had freaked out and was abandoning him, he dropped the carton of eggs on the counter, probably breaking half of them, and sprinted toward the exit.

"Mia?" he yelled.

But as he reached the front room, it wasn't Mia poised and frozen in the opened front door.

"Mia?" Amanda repeated harshly as she came the rest of the way inside. "Is that whose car is parked out front? I thought it looked familiar."

"Mandy." His jaw dropped. This was totally not how he'd wanted her to find out. He wasn't sure how exactly he wanted to break the news, but it definitely wasn't like this.

To make matters worse, Mia appeared at the top of the stairs, wearing nothing but his T-shirt he'd loaned her to wear to bed. Both siblings gawked up at her. Mia jerked to a halt as if she realized she'd caused a serious problem. Her eyes apologetically met Drew's.

"You traitor," Mandy hissed. She whirled around and slammed from the house.

"Mandy!" Drew hurried after her, not even feeling the gravel dig into his bare toes while he raced her across the drive. As she yanked the driver's side door open, he shoved it closed. "Please try to not fly off the handle," he panted out. "You know I'd never do anything to hurt you —"

"Then why are you?" she snapped, finally glancing at him to pin him with a glare.

He sighed, took a step back, and ran a hand through his hair. "I know you're going through a hard time. And I am going to be here for you. Anything you need, you know you can count on me."

She snorted and turned away, folding her arms over her chest. "Yeah, well, I needed you today. It's Jeffery's first weekend with the kids, and I'm all alone. I need . . ."

When he touched her shoulder, she jerked away from him. "Mandy," he murmured in soft reprimand. "Don't be mad at me. Don't . . . don't be upset just because I'm happy and you're miserable."

"I'm not," she muttered and whirled around to glare at him. "But why do you have to be happy with her?"

256

His jaw turned hard. "Mia isn't the one who was involved with Jeff."

Mandy's eyes frosted over. "No," she agreed in a tight voice. "But I bet she knew it was happening. I bet she listened to her little friend give all sorts of details about my husband. I bet she even —"

"That's enough," Drew said in a tight voice. "She couldn't help what her roommate was doing any more than I can help having you for a sister."

Amanda's jaw dropped and she stared at him with wide eyes.

He sighed, suddenly exhausted and rubbed at a spot on the center of his forehead. "Don't talk bad about her. I care about her, okay. I care a lot."

"You . . . what? No. Drew," taking his shoulders in her hands, his sister frowned at him and said, "You don't even know this girl. You've only met her what, three times?"

He glanced away, guiltily.

"Drew," Amanda whispered in horror. "You've been dating her behind my back. All this time. Haven't you?"

"I wouldn't call it dating," he answered. "We never actually went on a date." He winced. "Except maybe for the night we went out to eat pizza."

"You know what?" Amanda growled. "It

doesn't matter what you've been doing with her. Whatever it was, you've been doing it behind my back." Glowering, she asked, "Don't you even care how I feel about this?"

"Don't you care how I feel?" he countered.

"You're not thinking with your brain, so no, I don't care what you think you're feeling. It's not real. What's real is my problem. My divorce. And I need you, Drew."

He spread his arms wide. "Well, I'm right here for you. That's not going to change no matter who I'm dating."

"It matters to me," she shot back, pressing a finger against her own chest. "And if you love me at all, you'll tell her to leave right now. I won't come back here unless you get rid of her."

Drew swallowed. His throat burned and the words clogged in his windpipe. He wanted to beg his sister to understand, but in her current frame of mind, he knew she wouldn't. He would've liked to stand his ground and tell her he was with Mia now, and if she loved him at all, she'd deal with it. But once again, in her current frame of mind, that would only hurt her. So, he only managed to give a slight shake of his head, telling her he wasn't going to send Mia anywhere.

Amanda took a step back. Pressing her

hands to her chest, she turned away, muttering under her breath, "I have to go."

"You're the only person who has a problem with this, Mandy," he called after her.

Ignoring him, his sister climbed into her car and drove off.

He watched her go, wishing he could've concocted some magic words to ease her worries, anything but tell her the one thing she wanted him to say. There was no way he was going to leave Mia, though. Not now. Not even for his sister who was supposed to be the most important person in his world.

Turning away from the drive, he slumped back to the house. Mia pulled open the front door as soon as he started up the porch. Her eyes were huge and full of worry.

He slowed to a stop. "You heard?"

Her head bobbed up and down. Oh, yeah. She'd definitely heard. She'd heard his sister demand, loud and clear, that he wash his hands of her.

There was nothing he could say to assure her he wasn't going to take his sister's advice. She'd still have her doubts. So, he did the only thing he could think to do. Show her. He opened his arms.

The relief on her face was almost tangible. She flew at him, leaping into his embrace, winding her arms so tight around his neck, he wondered if they might need to use the jaws of life to pry her off.

"I'm sorry," she said, kissing his face and neck. "I'm so sorry."

"She'll get over it," he assured, rubbing a soothing hand down her back.

"But she needs her brother right now. She needs all the family she can get."

"Shh." To quiet her, he pressed his mouth to hers. Their lips clung a few seconds before he pressed his forehead to hers. "I know my sister. She'll get over her mad in a few hours. Then she'll call, and we'll be fine again. She'll be nice to you because she knows how important you are to me. And before you know it, she'll love you just as much as I do. So stop worrying. It'll be okay."

She trembled. It made him a little panicked. Hoping she wouldn't have an anxiety attack on him, he put his finger under her chin and lifted her face. "Mia?"

Tears swam in her eyes. But she smiled at him and he knew they were tears of joy when she added, "I love you too."

He sucked in a breath. Sweeping her into his arms, he carried her inside.

"Look who's coming home at ten in the morning after a two-day date."

Mia blushed and ducked her head. The front door slid closed at her back, and Piper let out a soft chuckle.

"I was worried the first night, not sure what had happened to you."

Face snapping up, Mia instantly apologized. "I'm sorry I didn't call. I totally forgot —"

Piper shook her head and lifted a hand. "Don't worry about it. Drew let me know where you were."

"He did?" Mia snapped her mouth shut, instantly jealous. As irrational as she knew it was, she still pictured her roommate pursuing Drew. If she dated married men, she wouldn't have any qualms about going after someone who was now considered unavailable. But then she straightened, telling herself how silly such a worry was. Piper was her best friend on earth; her best friend wouldn't mess with her man.

Still, why hadn't he told her he'd spoken to her roommate?

"The first night you didn't come home, I found his business card in your room and tried calling, hoping it was his personal number too."

"Oh," Mia said, realization dawning. "Was that you? I remember the phone ringing downstairs on his business line."

"That was me," Piper nodded and raised her hand to claim culpability. "I left a message and he called me back the next morning to tell me you were fine and not to ever call him again because his sister visited frequently."

Mia nodded, reassured. She should probably be irritated Drew had said such a thing to her best friend. But she kind of liked the idea that they weren't too close. She couldn't help but worry just a little about Piper trying to steal her man. Drew was too wonderful to lose.

"She does visit a lot," Mia assured Piper. "She showed up that morning and wasn't very happy when she found me there." Yet another reason Drew probably hadn't told her about his call to Piper. They'd been suitably distracted.

Piper gasped and covered her mouth with both hands. "Are you okay? What did she do?"

"She called Drew a traitor and stormed off. He's been trying to get in touch with her ever since. But she refuses to talk to him." Shoulders slumping, she admitted, "I feel sorry for her. She'd been betrayed by her husband and now her brother is fraternizing with someone she considers an enemy."

When she glanced toward Piper, she froze, realizing Amanda's problems started because of Piper. What a way to make her friend more guilty. She opened her mouth, mind whirling to cover her faux pas. "I mean —"

"No, it's okay," Piper assured her. "I feel bad for her too. J made her out to be the wicked witch of the west, but now that I realize how much he lied to me, she probably wasn't as bad as I imagined." She snorted sourly. "He ended up being the jerk and still . . . he's the one who dumped me."

Blinking rapidly, she glanced away, trying to hide her misery.

"I'm sorry," Mia said, feeling lame because, well, she wasn't actually that sorry her friend was no longer seeing a married man.

"It's fine," her friend said. "Actually . . . well, Gary called. We're going out this weekend."

Mia's eyebrows shot up. "Gary. The Gary I was supposed to go out with?"

Piper nodded, and Mia sat down.

She felt like she'd landed in a strange soap opera. There were definitely some odd triangles going on, er, actually this would be more like a hexagon since Drew, his sister, her husband, Piper, Gary and Mia were all involved. What a weird outcome.

"Still nothing?"

Drew hung up the phone, shaking his head. "It's been five days and she still won't talk to me. I've gone over there twice, both time when the kids were around, and she'll just walk into a different room whenever I enter one."

Mia sat on the arm of his couch and wrapped both her arms around him. "Are you okay?"

He touched her hand and closed his eyes. "Yeah." He was better than okay. Every time she was near he was fantastic.

Wanting to prove it, he turned and lifted his face to kiss her. She bent down to press her mouth to his. Afterward, he sighed and closed his eyes, holding her close, grateful she was in his life to help him deal with his troubles.

As if reading his mind, Mia placed her hand on his hair. "She'll call."

He murmured his agreement, hoping she was right, and feeling closer to her than ever because she was intuitive enough to realize how much Amanda's cold shoulder bothered him. Her understanding assured him he was still doing the right thing.

He tilted his head her way and kissed her again. "Thank you."

CHAPTER SEVENTEEN

The telephone woke Drew. It was early, too early for anyone to actually be awake. Groaning, he rolled onto his stomach and reached for the nightstand.

After a few blind sweeps with his hand, he answered in a sleep-filled voice, stretching so he barely heard his sister's voice over his own yawn. "Mandy," he mumbled, already sighing. "Not right now. It's —"

"Felix fell," she said, her voice was hoarse and shaky.

He opened his eyes. "What? What happened? Is he okay?"

"He won't wake up. Oh, Drew. I heard the bump in the kitchen and when I got there, he was lying like a little, limp rag doll in the middle of the floor. And I couldn't get him to wake up. My baby won't wake up."

Drew sat up quickly enough to make the blood rush to his head. Ignoring the dizzy spell, he yanked on a pair of pants. "Did you call an ambulance?"

"We're already at the hospital. Could you . . . could you please come get the girls. I don't want them here if . . ." Her voice broke.

"I'll be right there," he told her before hanging up.

He dialed another number as he reached for his shirt, not even thinking what he was doing until Mia answered.

He said her name. She must've heard the anxiety in his voice because her next words were, "What's wrong?"

"My nephew. He fell or something. I don't know. They're already at the hospital. I have to go."

Bypassing socks, he snatched a pair of forgotten shoes off the floor and hopped on one foot toward the door as he put them on.

"Do you want me to come with you?"

Dropping his lifted foot to the floor, Drew paused. He wanted her with him more than anything, but he shook his head. "You don't have to do that."

She'd freak out if she entered a hospital where she knew a little boy was hurt. And there was no telling how Mandy would receive her.

But Mia didn't seem to care about all that. "Do you want me there?" she asked, her steady voice calming him.

He did so bad it hurt. But there were so many problems with the idea, he couldn't answer clearly. He gave a mumbled, "Yes," and she answered, "Okay. Then I'm coming. Pick me up on your way. I'll be ready and waiting at the curb."

Drew froze a second before he closed his eyes and sighed. "I love you so much," he murmured.

"I love you too," she rushed out the words. He could hear her moving around in the background, probably hastily throwing on clothes like he'd just done. "Now hurry up and get over here."

Grinning, he disconnected and did just that.

By the time he pulled up in front of 410 South Elm, she was opening the door and hurrying outside and pulling the door shut behind her, still barefoot but carrying her shoes so she could put them on in the truck.

Grateful for her presence, he only managed one look her way as she hopped inside. Though her face was pale, she offered him a stiff, but encouraging smile. Knowing he could handle whatever happened with her next to him, he pulled onto the roadway.

■ ■ ■ ■

A hard ball of tension knotted her stomach as Drew parked next to the hospital's emergency entrance and beside a Honda Civic he claimed was his sister's. Fear nipped at her; she didn't want to step foot inside those automatic glass doors. Her daughter might not have died in a hospital and it had been too late to take her to one, but Mia knew there was a mother nearby, fearing for her baby's life. And that emotion was way too familiar.

As Drew rushed forward into the building, Mia hung back for two reasons. First, wicked memories were nearly smothering her . . . and then there was his sister. Mandy still refused to acknowledge her in Drew's life. Her hatred would only grow to new proportions if she was forced to see Mia right now at this awful moment.

Most likely realizing that fact himself, Drew paused and glanced behind him. When he saw her hanging back, he nodded in approval and gratitude. Then he turned back and hurried toward his sister.

"Mandy?"

She lifted her face, terror clutching her features and surged to her feet. "Drew!"

The relief in her voice made Mia love him all the more. People depended on him and were happy to see him, even in their darkest hour of distress.

Brother and sister stopped three feet away from each other.

"Have you heard anything?" he asked.

Mandy shook her head, looking hollow and alone. "No. Nothing."

Mia's heart went out to the bereft mother. Remembering all too clearly that lost, empty sensation, she set her hand over her churning stomach. About the time she whispered, "Hug her, Drew" under her breath, he pulled his sister into his arms. She swallowed with pride. "Good man."

Still holding Mandy closer, he asked, "Where're the girls?"

"I called Dad too," she said. "He offered to take them. Since he's only a few blocks away, he's been here and gone." Pulling back enough to give him an uncertain look, she said, "I was hoping you'd stay here . . . with me."

"Of course," he answered immediately, taking her hand to pull her down next to him on the cushioned chair, he kept a hold of her fingers. "I'm not going to leave you."

As Mandy rested her head on his shoulder and he began to sift his fingers through her hair, something powerful and achy moved through Mia. Keeping herself out of sight from Drew's sister, she continued to eavesdrop, unable to take her eyes off him. If only he'd been there after Lexie's death. He would've held her like that, comforted her. Maybe it wouldn't have taken her over three years to heal.

Realizing at that moment that she had indeed healed, she pressed a hand to her chest, and three years of pressure eased off her lungs.

"Where's Jeff?" she heard Drew ask.

Amanda shrugged, staring bleakly at a wall. "I called. Had to leave a message. Told him to call me back."

"You didn't tell him what happened?" Drew sounded incredulous.

His sister glanced over long enough to glare. "If he cares anything about his children, he better call back."

Drew pushed to his feet, running his hand through his hair. Digging his cell phone from his pocket, he began to dial. "I'll call him," he said and started to look around the waiting room as if looking for Mia.

She stepped into view and his eyes instantly darted her way. They exchanged a long look before he smiled and commenced to leave a message for Amanda's husband,

271

explaining everything that had happened. Mandy finally noticed her as Drew was hanging up and putting his phone away.

Straightening her back and narrowing her eyes, she hissed, "What is she doing here?"

"She's here for me," Drew answered, his tone leaving no room for question. He sat down next to Amanda not even glancing Mia's way as if he trusted her support that much.

But his sister didn't like his answer. Eyes filling with tears, she rasped, "I can't have her here right now, Drew. She reminds me of what he did. And I can't think about that. I can't . . ."

She shook her head, looking grey. "I've been thinking about it too much. That's why I was sleeping in this morning. I stayed up so late last night, thinking and stressing. And Felix knew I was upset. He woke me a few minutes before . . . before it happened and said he was going to make me breakfast. I stayed in bed. I was being lazy, and lying in bed when he crawled up onto the kitchen counters. He was so sweet, Drew. When he put his hand on my hair and told me he was going to bring me breakfast in bed because I didn't feel well."

She sobbed and Drew shuddered.

"Mandy, no." He reached for her, but Mia

272

was suddenly there.

She caught his arm. He whirled around to scowl at her, but when he saw the look in her eyes, he paused. She shook her head, and he gave a slight reluctant nod.

And all the while, Amanda kept talking, sobbing out the entire story. "The next thing I knew, he was screaming and then there was this thump. And suddenly everything went quiet. I found him lying in a pile of Fruit Pebbles. His favorite cereal. He was going to give me his favorite cereal for breakfast."

Hunching her shoulder to bury her face in her hands, she started to weep and didn't notice how Mia had urged Drew out of his seat so she could take his place beside Amanda. "I should've gotten out of bed. I shouldn't have let him know how miserable I was."

Mia set a hand on Amanda's back. "No, you should be proud of your son. He had the compassion to care for his mother when she needed someone to care for her."

Amanda lifted her face. The grief and tears had aged her since she'd bent over to weep. But anger quickly wiped away her anguish. She glared at Mia.

Mia swallowed but didn't back down, especially when Amanda growled deep in her throat in animalistic warning. "Don't you dare tell me how to feel." She vibrated with the force of her rage. "You don't know what I'm feeling. You have no idea what it's like to be responsible for your child's —"

"Mandy," Drew said, his voice reprimanding as he stepped forward to stop her.

But Mia lifted her hand and glanced his way. "It's okay," she told him. "This is good."

"Good?" Amanda roared, surging to her feet and fisting her hands. "You think it's good that my son is lying in some hospital bed, dying?" She shrank backward at her own words, covering her face with her hands and trembling.

"Yes, as a matter of fact, I think your anger is very good," Mia said, not wavering from her position in the chair. "It's a healthy step in the grieving process."

Amanda scowled. "What?" Tears matted her face, making her cheeks glow red. She wrinkled her features in confusion. "What are you? Some kind of quack?"

"No, I'm Mia Stallone," Mia answered, gracefully rising to her feet to face the other woman on the same level. "And I've been living through the stages of grief for three years, four months and two days."

Brows lowering in confusion, Amanda

274

merely stared, shaking her head.

Mia dragged in a deep breath and finished, "Ever since my three-month-old daughter suffocated to death while she was sleeping in bed next to me."

Amanda shuddered. "Oh. How horrible."

Nodding, Mia murmured, "Yeah. Pretty much." Collecting a brave breath, she glanced once toward Drew, and her chest eased. She turned back to his sister. "I was responsible for my child's pain . . . for her death. So, I know how you feel. I understand how much you hurt right now." Relaxing her tense shoulders, she reached out with one hand toward Amanda. "I understand," she repeated.

Blinking back a new flood of tears, Amanda let out a tortured moan and surged toward Mia, hugging her hard. "I don't want him to die," she said desperately, balling the back of Mia's shirt in her fists. "I just don't want him to die."

"He might not," Drew said, stepping forward to encompass both women in his arms.

Mia rested her head on his shoulder as she patiently stroked Mandy's hair. "There's still hope."

Drew pressed a brief kiss to their foreheads and pulled them tighter against him.

"I'm so scared," Amanda admitted weakly as she let Mia support her and Drew support them both.

Mia didn't answer and neither did he. She could tell he was just as worried as his sister was. She'd never met Felix, but she'd heard about him from Drew and seen his picture. She compared his vigor to Lexie's. It'd be awful if he was no longer around to cheer the world with his animated enthusiasm.

She closed her eyes tight and prayed, leaning against Drew the entire time. He rested his face on the top of her head, seeking as much as he gave.

From behind them, a trembling voice spoke. "A-Amanda?"

Drew's sister slowly pulled away from them, lifting her face. Her soon-to-be-ex-husband stood fifteen feet away, drawn and shaky, his lips pressed thin.

"Jeffrey?" Mandy rasped.

"Is he . . . is he . . . ?" he was too afraid to ask.

When she just stood there, probably too choked up to answer, Drew finally supplied, "We're still waiting for news from the doctor." Keeping his arms around Mia, he eased them both backward so Felix's parents could have room.

Jeff nodded, never taking his eyes from

Mandy. "Where are the girls? Are they okay?"

Instead of answering his question, Mandy murmured monotonously, "He fell. He . . . he was trying to make me breakfast, and he fell off the kitchen counter. He hit his head and wouldn't wake up. The doctor's still with him and . . . and it's all my fault. I wasn't there to stop him."

"No," Jeff breathed. "No, none of this is your fault. Amanda . . ." Tortured eyes lifted to hers. "I'm so sorry."

Mia had to look away when unashamed tears filled the man's eyes.

"I've made such a mess of everything," he choked out, bowing his head with shame. "This wouldn't have happened if I hadn't . . . if I hadn't . . ."

Pity filled Mandy's face. "Jeffrey," she murmured stepping close. She lifted her arms but dropped them at the last second.

"No," he said, obviously not caring for her resistance. He grabbed her wrist and tugged her into his arms.

She wilted once she was there, resting her head on his shoulder much like Mia had just done to Drew's.

"I love you," he said, kissing her hair and her cheek. "Everything will be okay. Felix will be okay. We'll be a family again, I swear.

Everything will be okay."

The litany seemed to calm his wife. Amanda closed her eyes and relaxed in his embrace, filling Mia with a spark of jealousy, even though she knew all the problems they had. In the face of tragedy, they clung together. Ryan had only pushed her away.

She glanced up at Drew and he seemed to sense her mood. He wrapped his arms around her tight and pressed his face into her hair. He gave her the comfort she'd needed three years ago . . . or maybe he was seeking his own comfort for his nephew. Either way, Mia accepted his embrace wholeheartedly.

"We'll work this out. I'll change. I swear," Jeffrey was murmuring to Amanda. "Everything will be okay."

Drew's arms tightened around Mia, and when she looked up, she saw a doctor in blue scrubs approaching.

"He's awake," the doctor said. A cry of gratitude that came from both of Felix's parents drowned out the rest of his words. They clutched each other hard and Drew kissed Mia's mouth. "He has a concussion but . . ." was about the only thing Mia heard over all the commotion. "You may go back to see him now."

Jeff and Mandy surged forward. Mia held

back with Drew. She looked up at him to see if he wanted her to stay behind since she wasn't family and she hadn't even met his nephew yet. But he looked just as uncertain about following them.

Amanda answered both their reservations when she paused and glanced back, waving them forward. "Drew. Mia," she beckoned.

Her husband must've finally realized Mia was present, because he faltered and gawked at her with recognition, glancing between her and Drew. She would've stayed behind at that but Drew tugged her forward, and she couldn't abandon him.

As soon as they reached the room, Mia hesitated outside the door. She wasn't used to such a happy ending. She wasn't used to the child making it through okay. Scared she might resent the fact little Felix was alive and Lexie wasn't, she wondered briefly if she should wait outside.

Drew didn't give her a choice. He plowed into the room, dragging her along behind him. He finally let go of his grip when he saw his nephew sitting up in bed sucking Sprite through a straw.

The boy looked healthy and alive and ready to tackle life. Relief spread through her, consumed by joy and thankful everything had worked out okay.

CHAPTER EIGHTEEN

Drew's warm hand squeezed around Mia's. "How're you doing?"

She lifted her face. After sitting and visiting with Felix and his parents for over an hour in the little boy's recovery room, they finally had their first moment alone in the hospital elevator where Drew watched Mia with concern clouding his eyes.

A consuming ball of love filled her. In the short time they'd been together, he'd come to know her better than anyone.

Her smile was soft as she squeezed his fingers in return. "I'm good. Actually, I'm better than good. I just had a huge development in my grieving process."

Dr. Higgins was going to be pleased. Her biggest fear had been sharing her story with someone else who had suffered through a similar misery. But today, she realized it was healing to share. When she'd held Amanda after telling her story, the release was overwhelming. She knew she could move on without the usual guilt of wanting to live again. She was liberated.

"Seeing such a terrible situation end up okay helped you realize there's still good in the world, huh?" Drew asked, leaning toward her to kiss her temple.

"There's that," she admitted. "Plus talking to your sister about Lexie helped me get through a very big step. I think . . . I know I'm going to be okay now."

He paused to let her precede him out of the hospital. "I knew you would be," he admitted, once again sidling beside her as they stepped outside. "But I'm glad you've realized it too."

They shared a smile and tightened their grip on each other. After walking her to his truck and opening her door for her, he hurried around to the driver's side and started the engine.

"I'm glad your nephew's going to be okay," she said. "He's a complete doll, you know. He looks a lot like you."

"He's usually more ornery. I could tell the fall hurt him because he was so calm today. But, yeah, I'm glad he'll return to his mischievous self."

"Lexie was active like that too," Mia admitted. She sighed with pleasure, realizing it didn't hurt to admit that fact. She could finally think back on her baby fondly.

"I always thought I'd end up with an energetic kid. Mandy used to say I was a terror on two legs when I learned to walk."

Tilting her head in curiosity, Mia eyed him across the cab of his truck. "You've thought about yourself with children?"

He went still, the expression on his face freezing before he slowly glanced her way. After a noncommittal shrug, he returned his gaze to traffic as he pulled out the hospital's parking lot.

His strange response made her frown. Did he want children?

Silence grew between them. Drew kept sending her probing glances as they neared his house. After he pulled into the drive and parked, he stayed seated, keeping his hands on the steering wheel and staring out at the pasture beside his place.

She held her breath, wondering what had just happened between them to put such a chill in the warm air.

"Are you okay?" she whispered as she set her hand on his knee. Her fingers trembled with uncertainty.

His smile was instant. "Of course," he said, taking her hand and immediately reassuring her with his warm grip. "I was so glad I had you there today. I'm glad you were with me."

"Oh," she answered, surprised by his sudden intense mood. "Well, no problem. I was happy to help any way I could."

He nodded. "I'm glad you've healed so much too. Glad you feel good about your progress."

She paused, realizing he was working his way up to saying something big. Tilting her head, she wondered . . .

"I love you, you know," he said.

He was so serious, she held her breath, thinking he was breaking up with her for some reason.

"I love you too," she answered breathlessly, bracing herself in case she needed to beg if he tried to end things between them.

"After today, I realized I don't ever want to be without you. I want to be able to hold you every time things get bad."

Joy bloomed inside her. "I'd like that too," she admitted.

Her eyes searched his. It still felt like there was a big "but" lingering after his adamant proclamation. As he turned to open his door, she couldn't take her eyes off the stiff set of his shoulders. Something was definitely bothering him.

She bit her lip, watching him as she followed him to his front door, replaying the last few minutes in her head. With a gasp of intuition, she realized everything had changed the moment she asked if he thought about having children.

Children.

Drew and children.

Afraid to broach the subject, afraid to learn how her own response to his answer would affect her, Mia paused inside his front door and stared around his studio. Ninety percent of the pictures he displayed centered around children.

Forgetting to breathe, Mia focused on Drew as he paused, realizing she wasn't following him. Eyebrows wrinkling in confusion, he came back to her. "What's wrong?"

"Do-you-want-children?" she blurted out, lumping all the words together as one instead of four so she couldn't chicken out before asking the entire question.

Drew froze in mid-step, staring at her with big eyes, still five feet away. She wished he would move closer. She wanted to reach out and touch him, comfort herself in case things went downhill from here.

"Well?" she rasped in a suddenly hoarse voice.

His Adam's apple worked. Then his mouth

moved. Finally, the words came. "I . . . do you?"

After a brief shake of the head, she answered, "I asked you first."

"That's not fair," he muttered on an irritated frown. "I just found you Mia. And I don't want to lose you. So whatever you want to do —"

"That's not what I asked." She winced, wishing he'd have said what was inside his heart. "I know what I want. I want to know what you want."

"I want you to be happy. And if you can't —"

"Drew," she started. But he held up a hand.

"It doesn't matter," he assured her. "Either way, I'll —"

"I think it does matter very much."

Drew let out a frustrated growl. "You see, there . . ." He pointed his finger at her, shaking it. "I can't answer you because it's a trick question. If I say something that's different than what you want and we decide to follow your decision, then you'll worry for the rest of your life that I'm not happy . . . and I am. I've never been this happy in my life. So, either way, I don't think I could be happier if we had a house full of twenty children."

"So you do want children?"

He blew out an agonized breath. "Mia," he said in a low, strained voice. "If you can't . . . I mean, if you don't want to after Lexie, I don't want you to feel obligated."

"Are you worried I'd kill our baby?"

His eyes widened. "What? No! Not at all. That's the last thing on my mind."

"So . . . have you ever pictured yourself as a dad?"

Looking more panicked than she ever remembered seeing him before, he whispered back his dreaded answer. "Yes. But it's not that —"

"This is a yes or no question, Drew," she said. "Just . . . yes or no."

"Fine," he answered defeated. Closing his eyes, he muttered, "Yes, I have pictured myself having children. Even more so lately — especially since I met you."

Since he wouldn't open his eyes, he wasn't able to see her blinding smile. "I think you'd make a wonderful father," she declared.

His lashes jerked apart, his gaze startled as he gawked at her. The air rushed out of his lungs and he breathlessly gasped, "You do? Does that mean . . . ?"

She nodded. "Yes! I think I'd like to sometime."

"Oh, Mia." He stared at her wide-eyed a

moment before the smile broke out on his face. Then he lunged at her, pulling her into a fierce hug. "Thank God," he murmured against her hair. "Thank God."

"I love you," she said.

"I love you too. This is going to work for us. We're going to be so happy."

She opened her mouth to agree, but he continued before she had a chance. And that was perfectly fine with her if he wanted to cut in because he said, "I want to marry you."

She froze. "You . . . really?"

He nodded and rubbed his thumb over the back of her left index finger as if imaging a ring there.

"I do," he said. "Really."

"Oh, Drew." She leaned over the center console into his arms. "I want to marry you, too."

He pulled her close and repeated, "I love you. I love you so much."

"I love you too," she answered, and meant it with all her heart.

ABOUT THE AUTHOR

The youngest of eight children, **Linda Kage** grew up on a dairy farm in the Midwest. She now lives in Kansas with her husband, daughter and nine cuckoo clocks. Linda is a member of Romance Writers of America and its local chapter, Midwest Romance Writers.

www.LindaKage.com

The employees of Thorndike Press hope you have enjoyed this Large Print book. All our Thorndike, Wheeler, and Kennebec Large Print titles are designed for easy reading, and all our books are made to last. Other Thorndike Press Large Print books are available at your library, through selected bookstores, or directly from us.

For information about titles, please call:
(800) 223-1244

or visit our Web site at:
http://gale.cengage.com/thorndike

To share your comments, please write:
Publisher
Thorndike Press
10 Water St., Suite 310
Waterville, ME 04901